Reconciled for Easter

NOELLE ADAMS

This book is a work of fiction. Names, characters, places, and incidents are the product of the author's imagination or are used fictitiously. Any resemblance to actual events, locales, or persons, living or dead, is coincidental.

Copyright © 2015 by Noelle Adams. All rights reserved, including the right to reproduce, distribute, or transmit in any form or by any means.

ONE

"Mia! Are you ready to go?" Abigail Morgan called out from the kitchen, trying to put dirty dinner plates into the dishwasher and send an e-mail from her laptop at the same time.

It was almost six already, and Abigail needed to leave for a work function in less than an hour. She still had to shower and dress—not to mention pull the house into some sort of order and make sure her daughter had everything she needed for the weekend.

Flustered and too hot in the stuffy house, Abigail finished typing a reply to her boss and pressed Send, hoping she hadn't spelled any words wrong. She finished loading the dishwasher before she set it to run. "Mia!" she called again. "What are you doing?"

She knew the answer before she heard the little voice reply, "Reading."

Abigail closed down her laptop and glanced over the counter. There were piles of books and mail and homework sheets scattered around but no crumbs or dirty pots and pans. Not too bad, considering.

Abigail picked up one of Mia's books and a well-worn stuffed dog from the kitchen table before she went into the living room to find her daughter curled up in a ball on the couch. Reading, of course.

"Are you packed and ready to go?"

Mia lifted reluctant blue eyes and peered at her mother through small, wire-framed glasses. "Yeah."

"You have clothes for tomorrow and your brush and toothbrush?"

"Yeah."

"You have panties?"

Mia rolled her eyes. She was only six years old, but she'd always been an oddly mature child—extremely smart, frequently shy, and scarily observant. She didn't have very many friends her own age, and she listed the postman, the old lady with the poodle next door, and the butcher at the grocery store as the people she liked to hang out with.

Sometimes Abigail worried about her, and sometimes she stared at her daughter in awe.

"Mom," Mia sighed, still focused on the pages of her book.

A couple of months ago, Mia had forgotten to pack panties for one of her visits with her father. This lapse in memory had necessitated some improvisation on the part of Abigail's estranged husband—something Abigail would prefer not to repeat.

"Did you pack panties?" Abigail asked again.

"Yes."

"Here's this book." Abigail crammed the chapter book she'd grabbed from the counter into Mia's purple case. "You're only halfway through this one. And you've got that one you're reading now. Did you bring a couple more? You know how sometimes you run out."

"I brought four books, and Daddy always gives me more."

"I know, but it's best if you bring enough for the whole weekend."

Mia devoured books, and her reading abilities were far more advanced than her age group. But more than once

Abigail had been surprised at what she'd found her daughter reading upon returning from weekends with her father.

Abigail reached over and smoothed down some flyaways in Mia's long reddish-blond braids. "All right. Put up your book. Your daddy will be here any minute."

"He might be late."

"He won't be late today," she said, hoping she was speaking the truth. Thomas was often late—sometimes so late Mia would decide he wasn't coming at all. He hadn't been late as much recently though, so Abigail could speak with some degree of confidence. "He said he would get here on time."

Mia wrinkled her nose. "You just want me to leave so you can go out to your dinner."

"Mia, you know that's not true." She squatted on the floor next to the couch and held her daughter's gaze. "You know I always miss you when you're gone."

The girl frowned but didn't argue.

Feeling a knot of worry tighten in her throat, Abigail asked, "Are you a little upset that I'm going to this dinner tonight?"

"No."

"Are you sure? We sometimes have dinner with people who might donate money to Milbourne House. It's part of my job. Is there anything you want to ask me about it?"

Mia's blue eyes were level and strangely wary. "Are you going to dinner with Mr. Foster?"

Abigail sucked in a breath at the implications of the question. "He'll be at the dinner, but there will be other people there too. We're not going to dinner together just by ourselves."

"Does he like you?"

"Does who like me? Mr. Foster? He's my boss. I think he likes me, but not in any special way."

Mia was still frowning.

"Why did you ask that, Mia? What are you worried about?"

"Are you going to date Mr. Foster?"

"No! No, of course not. I just work with him. I'm still married to Daddy. There's nothing for you to worry about with that."

"Oh." Mia swallowed and stared at Abigail blankly. "Okay."

Abigail searched her daughter's face and fought another swell of worry. Mia was so quiet and so reflective that it wasn't always easy to know what was going on in her mind.

"Mia, tell me if you're upset about anything." She reached out to stroke her daughter's pale cheek. "I always want to know. Even if it's not good."

"I'm not upset. It's okay." Mia smiled—a smile that broke out in sudden brightness.

Abigail reached over to hug the girl. Then she stood up and offered the stuffed dog, Mia's favorite toy. "All right. Here's Baxter. You don't want to forget him."

"Yeah."

"All right. Help me pick up a little so the place isn't such a mess."

Mia heaved herself up and stuffed her dog in her case. Then together they started picking up some of the toys, books, papers, and shoes that littered the floor. Sometimes Abigail felt waves of guilt and embarrassment when she looked at her messy house, thinking about what her mother or father would say if they saw it. But Abigail had been separated from her husband for almost fifteen months, so she worked full-time and had primary responsibility for Mia. Housekeeping was way down on her to-do list.

When she heard a knock on the door, she sighed in relief. At least Thomas had shown up on time.

"Let your daddy in, and I'll put this stuff up," Abigail said, trying to juggle an armful of junk they'd collected from the living room.

She didn't actually put it up. She just dumped it on the floor of her bedroom and shut the door.

She could hear Thomas's voice wafting through the hallway with Mia's happy giggle.

The girl loved her father. That was good. It was something Abigail had worked hard to maintain after the separation.

The separation had been bitter since Thomas had refused to accept it or even understand why Abigail wanted it at all. Part of her had been absolutely convinced that divorce was the only option, but she'd also been reluctant to give up on the marriage completely, so she'd agreed to wait a year before making any decisions. They'd spent a year trying to work out the problems between them to no avail until they'd both been so emotionally exhausted that even the counseling had been counterproductive. So they'd agreed to take a break for six months so they could rest and recover, and then they'd try counseling again. If they couldn't work things out at that point though, they would have to make a final decision.

Some of Abigail's friends and acquaintances thought she should have given up on the marriage long ago since a relationship that took so much work couldn't be worth it. And other friends and acquaintances thought she was selfish and unreasonable for separating from her husband at all and she should just live with a broken marriage because that was her duty.

Abigail wasn't satisfied with either of those answers. She kept praying that after the six-month break was over the right thing to do would be clearer.

She came out into the living room to find Mia and Thomas seated across from each other in exactly the same position, leaning forward with hands on lap. They appeared to be having an intense discussion.

"It's a work dinner," Mia was saying. "Mr. Foster will be there, but there will be other people there too. They're there to ask for money from the people for Milbourne House."

Abigail's chest tightened painfully as she heard her daughter's earnest declaration. Something was troubling Mia about Mr. Foster, and Abigail would need to talk to her about it again.

Thomas had come right from work at the hospital, so he wore trousers and a green dress shirt that brought out the color of his eyes. He was fit and attractive, with brown hair, well-chiseled features, a high forehead, and an intelligent mouth. He looked faintly tired, but he had ever since she'd known him.

"I see," Thomas said, his eyes focused on their daughter. "Do we know where they're going?"

"We don't know," Mia answered.

"We're going to Spencer's," Abigail said, hoping Thomas's skeptical tone didn't mean he was still unhappy about her job.

He'd never wanted her to take this job to begin with. He'd hadn't even wanted her to work outside the home, although he'd said he wouldn't stand in her way.

He hadn't seem to resent it so much lately though, so she told herself she was misreading his tone. She smiled at him in greeting and then at Mia. "They have really good coconut pie at Spencer's, so maybe I'll get some for dessert."

"Yummy!"

"How was work?" Abigail asked, studying Thomas's face and thinking he looked more tired than normal. The creases between his brows were more pronounced than usual, and the expression in his eyes looked far too tense. He was a surgeon. When he'd had a bad day, it was usually a *really* bad day.

She hated the thought of it. Despite everything they'd gone through, she still couldn't help but want to take care of him.

"It was okay."

When she peered at him closely, he seemed to recognize why. His face changed, and he added in a soft murmur, "Really. It was fine."

Relieved, she glanced at the clock and gasped when she saw how late it already was. "Okay. I hope you both have a great weekend. Mia is all ready to go."

"Daddy said he's going to take me to play with Ellie and Aunt Lydia and Uncle Gabe tomorrow morning," Mia announced, scrabbling off the couch.

"That sounds like fun. Here's your case." Abigail picked up the lavender vinyl bag and handed it to Thomas. "You have everything, Mia? What about your outfit for the recital tomorrow?"

Mia's forehead wrinkled as she thought soberly over her worldly possessions. "I forgot my ballet shoes."

Abigail stifled a flutter of impatience—she had to take a shower soon if she was going to be ready on time—and she said with another smile, "Well, run get them so you and Daddy can get going."

Mia scampered out of the living room, and Abigail turned to Thomas, who was looking at the book Mia had been reading earlier. "She's eaten a light supper already since she was getting hungry."

"Okay," Thomas murmured. "Have you looked at this book?"

Abigail glanced at the cover. It was one of a series of popular children's books about a school for fairies. "Yeah. She got it from school. All the girls like them. It's kind of silly, I guess."

"It's terrible. Do they really think girls have to read something this shallow and superficial?"

"I talk about it with her," Abigail said, hoping Thomas wouldn't start blaming her for a badly chosen book. "She's read all the good children's books that I'm familiar with. I try to find her better stuff, but there's really not much out there, and she reads so quickly. She's just six, so I really don't think she should be reading Hemingway."

Thomas's eyes narrowed. "You know she just happened to pick that up—"

"I know," Abigail replied, keeping her voice quiet so Mia wouldn't hear. "But I think we should be careful about what she reads at this age. She'd not old enough to tackle adult subject matter. So all that's left is the fairy school. For now, at least. I don't think they're going to make her silly and shallow. She just needs stories to read."

"I'm sure we can find better books than this."

"I don't know. Maybe. But for now, this was the best I could find." She felt a familiar swell of guilt and defensiveness—both at the same time. She'd felt that way so often when she and Thomas had been together, and it never seemed to go away. She fought the instinct to snap at him so the conversation wouldn't turn into an argument. "If you can find something better, that would be great. Just as long as it's a children's book."

"Okay." Thomas glanced away from her, his shoulders a little stiff. "I will."

He was annoyed. Maybe at her or maybe just at the book. Abigail had been married to him for more than seven years, but sometimes even she had trouble reading his body language.

She was suddenly so tired that her knees threatened to buckle. Even in such a little thing, their inclination was to argue, and it took so much work not to do so.

There never seemed to be an end of the work their marriage required.

Mia came running out with her ballet shoes, and Abigail shook the thought away.

When they reached the door, she knelt down to give her daughter a big hug. "You have a good time. I'll see you at the recital tomorrow." She glanced up at Thomas. "She needs to be there by four."

Thomas lifted his eyebrows. "I have it in my schedule."

"You call me whenever you want to," Abigail told Mia. "I'll always have my phone on."

"I know." Mia pushed her glasses up more securely on her little nose.

"I'll see you tomorrow," she said to Thomas, who had hooked the strap of Mia's case on his arm. The little purple case was weirdly incongruous next to his well-tailored clothes and cool composure, and the contrast was so unexpectedly endearing that her heart contracted briefly. "You'll be staying for the recital?"

Thomas's mouth tightened. "Of course."

There was no "of course" about it. For the first few years of Mia's life, Abigail had fought a futile battle to get Thomas to prioritize his wife and daughter. It never happened. He'd been starting a surgical residency at Duke when they'd met. His work as a surgeon was stressful and consuming—no doubt about that—but it had slowly become the priority in his life. Abigail had spent so many nights crying alone in their bed that she still ached at the memories.

She'd kept hoping things would change when his residency was finally over since they'd been making plans to move to Willow Park where he could work at a small, relatively low-stress hospital. Her own education was kind of piecemeal, with graduate work in both Appalachian studies and historic preservation. So when she'd been offered her current job—at an historic estate in the mountains of North Carolina—she'd felt like it was a gift.

It wasn't far from Willow Park, where Thomas had grown up, and they'd planned to settle down here since it seemed best for the entire family, even though he'd been getting multiple offers from much more prestigious hospitals.

But then he had changed his mind. He'd decided not to move here. He hadn't wanted her to take the job—or any job, for that matter. His career had been more important than anything she and Mia needed from him. He hadn't been willing to budge in the slightest way, and he refused to acknowledge she might have reason to be upset by it.

That had been the last straw in their marriage.

Given his history, anyone might doubt his attendance at his daughter's ballet recital the following day.

She reminded herself he'd been trying harder lately, and then she gave him a little smile, which he returned.

With that little tension smoothed over, she tried to shoo them out the door since she was running very late now. She almost groaned when Thomas began an extended conversation with Mia in the doorway about her sparkly new shoes, and she had to physically push him outside when he stopped to take a call before he'd fully left the house.

Finally, she got them on their way, and she ran for the bathroom, having only a half hour to shower, dry her hair, apply makeup, find something to wear, and get dressed before she left.

If she didn't know better, she would have said that Thomas had been stalling on purpose, but he wasn't a petty man.

Abigail had met him when she was a senior in college. He'd been several years older, and they'd both been attending a very small conservative church. Back then, Abigail had still been trying to please her authoritative father, who had picked out that church for her to join when she'd started college. As soon as Thomas showed up one Sunday morning, the whole church seemed to decide almost immediately that the two of them should get together.

She'd thought Thomas was the smartest, funniest, most attractive man she'd ever met, and she'd been shocked and delighted when he seemed to want to get to know her. They shared the same faith, and for a while they seemed to want the same things out of life. They'd started dating as soon as she graduated from college, and they were engaged shortly afterward.

Not long into the marriage, Abigail had realized that Thomas wanted something very different from the wife than she could be to him.

When she got out of the shower, she dried off and went to get underwear out of her top drawer, noticing the framed picture she'd stuck in there because she didn't know what else to do with it.

She pulled it out now, looking at her and Thomas on their wedding day. Thomas had been skinnier then, not yet fully filled out after his scrawny boyhood, but mostly he looked the same. Her eyes lingered on his familiar face and the affectionate, almost protective look in his eyes.

She wanted him to look at her that way again. She wanted to feel the way she had that day, believing she could trust him completely, give herself to him completely, know he would never let her down. She'd been convinced there was no other man in the world as brilliant and funny and dear as he was.

She still believed that. If only they could live together.

Her eyes shifted over to her own image in the picture. Thomas might still look mostly the same, but she didn't look the same at all.

Her light brown hair had never been cut back then since her father hadn't allowed it, so it was long and thick and a little frizzy. She hadn't worn any makeup—even on her wedding day—and she'd been wearing her glasses since her father hadn't approved of contacts either. Her mother had made the dress, and it was pretty and modest and old-fashioned.

She looked like a different person now, with shoulder-length hair, contacts, makeup, stylish clothes, a career, and a lot more confidence. She felt like she was finally really *Abigail*.

Her father hadn't said a word to her since she'd walked out on Thomas. That was to be expected. But the thing that hurt the most was that Thomas had evidently only wanted the sheltered, compliant girl in this picture and not the woman she really was.

There was nothing to do but accept it. She'd spent so many years of her life anxious, self-conscious, and paralyzed by feelings of never being good enough. God had taken her through that, and she wasn't going to return to that place—not even to get her husband back.

Abigail was twenty-eight now. Once their six-month break was over, they would start to work on their marriage again, hopefully no longer too exhausted to invest in the process.

And part of her still hoped that, one day, Thomas would want who she really was as his wife.

∼

The following day, Abigail sat a railroad crossing, waiting for a slow-moving train to pass so she could get to the highway.

If it didn't clear quickly, she was going to be late for Mia's ballet recital.

Torn between cursing the train and praying for it to hurry up, Abigail was also thinking about texting Thomas to make sure he'd gotten Mia there all right and on time.

She didn't want to nag, but she also didn't want anything to go wrong.

Before she could make the decision, her phone rang. She hesitated when she saw who was calling, but she ended up connecting the call. "Hello."

"Hi, Abigail. It's Jessica Duncan. Daniel's wife?"

Abigail knew who Jessica was. She'd met the other woman several times when Mia had participated in children's events at Willow Park Presbyterian, Thomas's hometown church. Jessica was the wife of the pastor.

It was the church Abigail would have joined had Thomas not already had first rights to it.

"Hi, Jessica." Abigail smiled into the phone since she'd always liked the other woman. "How are you?"

"I'm fine. Am I catching you at a bad time?"

"No, no. I'm waiting for a train. I've got nothing to do but mutter under my breath."

Jessica laughed. She was quiet and intelligent and reserved, but she had a really good sense of humor.

"Oh, you had a baby recently," Abigail said as she remembered. "How is everything?"

"Great. His name is Nathan. We haven't gotten any sleep for a month, but otherwise things are going well."

"That's great."

"Anyway, I don't want to keep you long from your muttering. I was actually wondering if you would be interested in joining a book club I'm in with some other women. We've lost a couple of members, and I immediately thought of you."

Abigail was taken aback by the invitation since she'd on purpose avoided socializing with people she considered part of Thomas's circle. He had his own life, and she wanted to give him his space to make sure he didn't think she was intruding. "Oh. I... I don't know. What is it like?" She was mostly stalling for time, trying to think of a good excuse that wouldn't hurt anyone's feelings.

"We meet once a month. We read all different kinds of books—not just normal book-club books. And not everyone always reads the whole book each month, so it's fine if you get busy. It's just fun to get together. We have snacks and dessert and wine. We have a really good time, and we'd love if you could join us."

"How many people are in it?"

"Not too many anymore. Just me and Alice Duncan—Micah's wife—do you know her?" When Abigail said she did, Jessica continued, "Sophie Miller. You might not have met her yet. Oh, and Lydia is it in too. That's all for now. It's a good group, and I think you'd fit in."

"I don't go to the church or anything—"

"That's totally fine. It's not a church thing. It's just a group of us talking about books."

Abigail actually thought she might enjoy the book club, but she always felt a bit awkward around people who were close to Thomas. In another situation, they probably could have been her friends.

But both parts of a separated couple couldn't really be part of the same circle of friends, and this had been his community first. Plus she was the one who had left Thomas.

"You can think about it if you need to," Jessica said, evidently recognizing her hesitation and kindly giving her a way out. "I'll e-mail you the information if that's okay, and you can let me know."

"That would be great," Abigail said, relieved at the reprieve. "Thank you so much for inviting me."

"Of course. I really hope it works out for you to join us."

As she hung up, Abigail sighed and closed her eyes since there was no sign of the end of the train yet.

She would have loved to go to the church in Willow Park. It was the only church of her denomination within a half hour of where she lived. The people felt like her kind of people, and Daniel was an excellent preacher.

Instead, she was attending a church down the road. The teaching was solid, and the people were nice, but it still kind of felt like she was visiting there. She was so busy with her job and Mia that she'd never really gotten involved. She was just as committed to her faith as she'd always been, but some weeks, she didn't even go to church.

Her father would have strongly disapproved of her church attendance.

She pushed the thought from her mind since she was determined not to be constantly shaped by her insecurities from the past.

If things started to go better with Thomas, she could join the Willow Park church too. And if that never happened, she could be happy where she was.

This was the life she'd chosen to have, and it wasn't a bad one. It wasn't perfect, but nobody's was. Better to be Abigail, even without a husband, than to be who she'd been before.

~

Twenty minutes later, she rushed into the crowded auditorium, checking her watch for the twentieth time. Two minutes until four o'clock.

She'd barely made it in time for Mia's ballet recital.

Breathlessly, she scanned the rows of seats filled with chattering parents, searching futilely for an empty place with a decent view of the stage. Mia's lessons were given by the only ballet school in the county, so the recitals were always dreadfully long and very well attended. The auditorium was packed.

Abigail let out a relieved sigh when she saw Thomas's distinctive profile and forehead.

Despite the milling crowds, he'd seen her and was gesturing her over toward the front.

She hurried down the aisle and shook her head in dry amusement when she saw that he'd managed to snare two of the best seats in the house. Near the front but not so close you had to crane your neck to see the stage. And on the side aisle where it was easy to duck out to run to the bathroom or stretch your legs.

The seat next to him was empty. She didn't know if he'd been saving the seat for her or if he'd pretended it was taken so he wouldn't have to sit next to anyone. Either way, it was really nice of him to let her have it.

She smiled at him gratefully as she climbed over his legs to sit down. "Thanks." Then she noticed that in the next seats were his sister, Lydia, and her husband, Gabe. "Hi, there," she told them with a grin.

She liked Lydia, who was a no-nonsense, forthright kind of woman. She was the kind of woman Abigail always tried to be now—confident and sure of herself. Lydia had married Gabe just last fall, so Abigail had only met him once or twice before.

"Is Ellie nervous about the recital?" she asked.

Ellie was Gabe's daughter from his first marriage—a few years older than Mia—but she took ballet lessons from the same school.

"Yeah. She's so competitive that she's afraid she won't do better than all the other girls in her class." Lydia smiled, obviously finding this trait in her stepdaughter funny and understandable both.

"She's not afraid of messing up," Gabe added with a slow smile. "Just that she won't be the best."

Abigail laughed and said, since it was on her mind, "I was just talking to Jessica on the phone. She invited me to your book club."

"Oh," Lydia said. "That would be perfect! We're in desperate need of new blood there. I'd love if you can come. Do you think you can join?"

For some reason, Abigail was intensely conscious of Thomas's eyes on her profile as she replied, "I don't know. I said I'd think about it."

"I really hope you do. I know you have to take care of Mia, but she could probably come over and stay with Ellie if Thomas was busy, or—"

Lydia broke off when Gabe nudged her gently with his foot. "Maybe give her some breathing space," he murmured.

"I am," Lydia looked surprised and then apologetic. "I mean, I'm sorry. I didn't mean to be pushy or anything. I just think it's a great idea. Gabe's always telling me that not everyone wants me to organize their life for them."

"And then she tells me that organizing mine is a full-time job," Gabe added. He had a very attractive aura of laidback confidence, and it wasn't hard to see that he adored his wife.

Abigail smiled again, hiding a little twinge of jealousy. It would have been so nice to have the kind of marriage that Lydia and Gabe evidently had—where they helped each other and supported each other at the same time, where they didn't seem to have to struggle for every step forward they took.

She'd always wanted that. She still did.

She turned back to Thomas, who'd been listening to the conversation and who was the only one of the four not smiling.

"Everything all right?" he asked, his eyes scanning her face.

"Yeah. Just a hair appointment that ran over, and then I got stuck by a slow-moving train. How's Mia?"

"She's fine. She is a little nervous about messing up, I think."

Abigail nodded and lowered her voice as the lights began to dim. "Yeah. She's been nervous all week. Not that she'll admit it." She slanted Thomas a wry look. She knew exactly from whom their daughter had gotten the sometimes-frustrating unwillingness to admit anxiety.

Thomas turned to focus on the stage as the performances began, but he was visibly hiding a smile that filled her with warmth and flushed her cheeks.

Mia had a small part in the big number that began the recital, so Abigail watched as her daughter—pretty in pink taffeta and infinitely grave—lined up with the other small girls to perform a few simple steps and some arm gestures as background to the older dancers at the center of the stage.

"She didn't mess up at all," Abigail whispered, leaning over toward Thomas and speaking into his ear so as not to disturb anyone else. "Most of the other girls did. Did you see?"

The corner of Thomas's mouth quirked up. "I saw." He didn't make as much of an effort to keep his voice down as she had.

Leaning over, she whispered, "Her hair looks really good. Who did it?"

Mia's hair had been braided up and twisted prettily around her head, a much more sophisticated hairdo than anything Abigail ever had time for.

Thomas shook his head and mouthed out, "Shh." Then he acted like he was absorbed in the middle school–age girls dancing a routine as a flock of birds.

"Who did her hair?" Abigail repeated in a hushed voice. She was leaning over toward Thomas and was suddenly conscious of his clean, masculine scent and the way his shirt draped smoothly over his broad shoulders. "Was it your mom?"

Thomas murmured an incoherent response that she took for an affirmation. He was close to his parents, which Abigail had always been happy about since it was good for him and good for Mia too. She was particularly glad about this fact because the Morgans were currently the only set of active grandparents Mia had.

The recital went on forever. Mia's main routine was in the middle of the recital. It was the one her class had been working on for months. When her daughter appeared on stage, Abigail leaned forward, holding her breath eagerly as she waited for the music to begin.

Mia went through the steps flawlessly, with all the conscientious precision and dedication with which she approached every challenge. The expression on her face was sober and cautious, and she didn't miss a single turn of her toes or wave of her hand.

She also didn't exhibit any real sense of grace or artistry. And as proud as Abigail was, it was more than evident that Mia wasn't cut out to be a dancer.

When the little girls filed off the stage, Abigail turned to Thomas with a grin. But she blinked when she saw he was frowning.

"What?" she asked.

With thoughtful eyes still resting on the empty stage, Thomas murmured, "She doesn't like it."

"What?" With effort, Abigail kept her voice low since a new troupe of dancers was lining up to begin the next number.

"She doesn't like to dance. She did everything perfectly, but she's not having any fun."

"She might not be naturally inclined in that direction, but that doesn't mean she doesn't like it."

Thomas's frown deepened as he met her eyes. "You saw her face just now. She's not having fun. Why did you enroll her in the class?"

Now that she understood the direction of Thomas's concerns, Abigail experienced a rise of defensiveness. "If she really doesn't like it, she doesn't have to take another class." Her glare was cool, although her cheeks were burning the way they always did when she felt like she'd done something wrong. "But I like to give her as many kinds of experience as possible so she can branch out from always reading and see what else she's good at."

"Nothing's wrong with reading."

"I know that. I'm happy she's such a great reader. But she reads all the time. And she doesn't have very many friends. And she's really, really shy with kids her own age. I want to make sure she has a lot of social experience so she feels more comfortable. So I enrolled her in the dance class. I thought it would help. I'm sorry if you think I'm torturing the poor thing by making her take a class she doesn't like."

Abigail said far more than she had intended. She usually didn't lose control around Thomas anymore—she'd been doing better since they'd given themselves the break—and her emotional response worried her. She really didn't want to get insecure like this again. She really didn't want them to start fighting again.

She pulled away from him and stared blindly at the back of the woman's head in front of her, almost shaking with emotion. She was still anxious about parenting, and sometimes she felt overwhelmed with the pressure of having to do so much of it on her own. She loved Mia so much and thought she was so special.

But sometimes she thought toward the future with an ache of dread. And she imagined her smart, shy little bookworm in middle school and high school. During her own school-age years, Abigail had always felt isolated and mocked because of her old-fashioned clothes and strict upbringing. She didn't want Mia to experience anything like that.

Thomas adjusted beside her, draping his arm over the back of her seat. He wasn't putting his arm around her. In fact, he was probably just bracing himself so he could lean over and talk into her ear. But he suddenly felt close to her. His arm brushed against her shoulders.

A year ago, she would have jerked away from his touch.

"Abigail," Thomas murmured, his voice a little thicker than usual and his breath blowing against her ear. "You're doing a great job with Mia. I never meant to imply anything else."

"I know," she said with a hard swallow. "I just worry sometimes."

Thomas hadn't pulled back. He was still very much invading her personal space. "I don't think you need to worry about this. Not everyone has to be popular in school. That's pretty minor in the big picture. We make sure she's happy and secure about the important things, and let everything else fall where it does."

Abigail had no idea how he'd read her mind so precisely. With a little hitch in her breath, she turned to gaze up at him. Their faces were only inches apart, and the look in his eyes was intimate. Certain. Strangely reassuring.

It had been a long time since she'd felt that kind of support from Thomas, and the resulting emotion caused her vision to blur, smudging the lines of his handsome features. "Yeah," she breathed.

Even she wasn't sure if the word was an agreement or a question.

"Yeah," Thomas said, his face momentarily drifting even closer to hers.

The deep expression in his eyes took her off guard, and she jerked her head away to focus back on the stage, her breathing a little faster than usual.

There might still be hope for their marriage. But even if there wasn't, they could still work together as parents for Mia. He loved their daughter just as much as she did.

The idea made Abigail feel so much better—like she wasn't entirely alone.

Thomas smoothly retrieved his arm from the back of her seat and pulled out his phone again. Wanting to make sure he knew she appreciated his support, she reached over and put a hand on his knee.

When his eyes darted over to her questioningly, she murmured, "Thank you."

He twitched his eyebrows in ironic response.

Abigail managed to make it through the rest of the recital without falling asleep, and Mia had a small part in one more routine near the end.

When it was over, she and Thomas went to find Mia. The girl ran toward them as soon as she spotted them, and Abigail sank down to give her a big hug, raving about how wonderfully she'd done.

Mia beamed and squirmed appreciatively and then turned a little hesitantly toward Thomas like she wasn't sure what his reaction would be.

"Absolutely perfect," he said, with impressive gravity. When Mia giggled and threw herself at him, he leaned over and picked her up into an affectionate hug.

Abigail watched as her husband embraced their daughter, holding her tightly with naked tenderness as if the girl was precious. She felt deeply touched and a little confused.

Only recently had Thomas had started hugging Mia like that. He rarely had when they were together. He'd always been too busy and distracted with work, and even his physical affection had been minimal.

But sometime during the past year, that had clearly changed.

Still held in her father's arms, Mia turned back to look at Abigail. "We're going out for pizza!"

Abigail grinned. "Sounds yummy. I hope you have a really good time." Thomas's weekend with Mia didn't end until the next day, so Mia's supper plans were his decision.

Mia's beaming smile faltered as Thomas put her back on the ground. "You're going to come with us, aren't you?"

"Oh," Abigail said, with a pang of anxiety. She hated to crush her daughter's bright mood. "It's your time with your daddy tonight."

Her worried gaze alternating between Thomas and Abigail, Mia said, "But Daddy said you could come with us."

"Only if Mommy doesn't have other plans," Thomas put in softly.

Abigail's eyes flashed questioningly to Thomas, seeking affirmation that the invitation to join them was genuine. When he nodded in answer to her silent question, she smiled at Mia. "I can't think of anything I'd rather do than have pizza with you."

"Do you see how pretty my hair is?" Mia said, twirling around so Abigail could admire her hairstyle.

"It's gorgeous."

"Daddy did it for me. It took him *ages* to get it right!"

Abigail gasped in shock at this piece of information and cut her eyes back to Thomas.

But he was pretending he'd gotten a call.

TWO

Abigail was wiping her kitchen counter on Sunday when she noticed that it was almost nine o'clock.

She dried off her hands and walked down the hall to glance into Mia's room. The girl was already in bed, under the covers and holding a book up as she read.

"Did you brush your teeth?" Abigail asked, coming into the room and sitting on the edge of the bed.

"Yes." Mia was usually good about going to bed on time because that meant she got to read without interruption.

"Are you going to say good night to me, or should I slink off, despairing that my Mia wouldn't give me a kiss?"

The girl snorted and laid down her open book on the bed beside her. "Don't be silly, Mommy."

Abigail chuckled and leaned down to pull Mia into a hug, exhaling with affection as the little arms wrapped around her neck tightly.

"So you had a good weekend with Daddy?" Abigail asked as she straightened up.

"Yes. We had fun. He told me next time we could go to a big bookstore in Dalton and pick out books."

"That will be a lot of fun. There's a great big one there. So this weekend, you went to see Ellie and then had your ballet recital and then went out to dinner with me and Daddy. What else did you do this weekend?

"He made pancakes," Mia said, her sober face starting to glow as she remembered. "They were great big, and he made faces on them. One of them looked like Baxter!" She held up her favorite stuffed dog to emphasize her point.

"He did?" Abigail couldn't help but smile at her daughter's obvious delight at the memory. "Did he use chocolate chips and whipped cream to make the faces?" For a moment, she wanted so much to be part of the pancake-making episode that her chest ached with the feeling. Thomas was usually a very serious man, so the times he relaxed and had fun had always meant so much to her. She could picture his smile even now, and she felt a pull of longing so strong it took her breath away.

She was convinced the break they were taking was a good thing for both of them. She was starting to feel refreshed, like she might have the energy to tackle their relationship again.

But she hadn't seen him much lately because of it, and she missed him.

Mia hadn't noticed her distraction and was answering the question happily. "No. I wanted whipped cream, but he said it would mess up the faces. He used blueberries and strawberries and dried cranberries and raisins and pieces of this orange fruit." Her forehead wrinkled. "I don't remember what it was called. He said it grew in tropics."

Abigail hazarded a guess. "Mangoes?"

Mia gave a satisfied nod, her glasses slipping down her nose. "Yes. Mangoes." She giggled. "They were funny faces. He made one that looked like you."

"He did? Did it have a big nose and funny hair?"

"No," Mia said, frowning disapprovingly. "It was pretty. We both thought so."

Abigail felt another emotional tug at the idea that Thomas still thought she was pretty—even her representation on a pancake. "What else did you do besides eating pancakes?"

"We read a lot. We read two whole books. Long ones!"

"What do you mean 'we'? He read them too?"

Mia huffed like her mother was being dense and slow. "Yes, he read them. We read them together. He reads, and then I read."

Abigail blinked, vaguely baffled by the incongruous picture her daughter's words evoked. "You mean you read them out loud?"

"Yes. That's how we read."

Swallowing, Abigail tried to process what she'd heard. She was so overwhelmed by the knowledge that Thomas had starting sitting with his daughter and reading for hours that her vision blurred over briefly.

He hadn't come home until after bedtime on Mia's third birthday, causing the girl to cry herself to sleep. Sometimes when they'd been together, days had gone by when he hadn't seen his daughter at all because of his long hours at the hospital. He hadn't wanted to take his current position, even though his work schedule would be much less stressful and he'd have a lot more time for family, because it wasn't as impressive a step in his career.

He'd ended up taking it anyway, but that was after their marriage had already crashed and burned. And he'd made it very clear that he was taking it begrudgingly and resented Abigail for making him do it.

The knowledge that he'd changed—that he was trying so hard and keeping it private so she wouldn't even know—meant so much to her that she literally started to shake.

"Are you okay, Mommy?" Mia asked.

Abigail quickly pulled herself together, not wanting Mia to get concerned. "Yes, I'm okay."

Mia had obviously been doing some thinking of her own. "Do you think Daddy loves me more now than when I was little?"

Abigail tensed up and focused again on Mia, who was frowning thoughtfully. "What? Why do you ask that, sweetie?"

"Because he seems to love me more now."

Evidently, Mia's thoughts had gone down the same paths as Abigail's, but the girl was even less equipped to understand the transformation than Abigail was.

With a catch in her throat, Abigail gathered her daughter into a tight hug. "No, baby. He's always loved you. Daddy has always loved you so much."

"But he didn't used to hang out with me." Mia snuggled against her, not trying to pull out of the embrace like she sometimes did.

Abigail took a minute to control her emotions. She tried so hard to make sure her baby was perfectly safe, perfectly happy, perfectly loved, but there was so much she couldn't control. Turning that control over to God where her daughter was concerned had always been a struggle for her, and it didn't get any easier as Mia got older.

"Daddy has a very hard job," Abigail said, making her voice as gentle as she could, praying she was handling it right. "Sometimes it takes all his time. He always wants to hang out with you as much as he can. But even when he can't, he still loves you. He always loves you, sweetie. And if sometimes he can't spend as much time with you, he still loves you."

"I don't think he will."

Abigail actually gasped. "You don't think he will love you?"

"No." The girl looked at her like she was being silly again. "I don't think later on he'll stop hanging out with me."

Abigail tried to answer but couldn't, suddenly wishing Thomas was here too. He always seemed to know what to do in tricky situations like this. He was smarter than anyone she'd ever known.

"Daddy likes to hang out with me," Mia added, as if her earlier point needed more explanation. "And he's not as sad as he used to be."

"What do you mean? When was he sad?"

"Before," Mia explained, waving her hand as if that was plenty of explanation. "But he's not like that anymore."

Abigail's head was spinning with so many questions and feelings she had no way of sorting them out. Afraid that if she spoke she would say something stupid, something she couldn't take back, she decided to let the subject go until she'd thought through the best way to handle it.

She leaned down to give Mia a kiss on the forehead. "Daddy loves you so much. Just like me. I'm glad you had a good time with Daddy."

Mia sighed happily. "Me too."

They said their regular nighttime prayers together, and then Abigail stood up. "Turn the light off at nine thirty. I'll come to check."

When Mia held up Baxter, Abigail gave the stuffed dog a kiss. "Good night, Baxter." Then she leaned down to kiss the little mouth Mia was pursing up expectantly. "Good night, Mia."

"Night night, Mommy."

Abigail left the room, her feelings in an uproar. She had no idea what to think about so much of the discussion she'd just had with her daughter.

She almost called up Thomas right then—since she wanted so much to hear his voice—but she stopped herself. They were obviously both really trying to work on their personal issues during their break, and she didn't want to mess things up by moving too quickly.

There were so many lingering difficulties between them, and if their marriage and their history had taught them anything, it was that simply trying wasn't always enough to mend what was broken.

~

"Mommy! Daddy's here!" Mia's shout from the living room carried through the house to Abigail's bedroom, where she was staring into her closet.

"I'm coming," Abigail called back. "Don't open the door unless you know for sure it's him."

"I heard his voice. He told me through the door."

"All right. You can let him in. I'll be there in a minute."

Abigail dug through the clothes that were stuffed into the not-large-enough closet. There had to be something she could wear for her function tonight that would make her look respectable.

Her bed was piled with outfits she'd already tried on and discarded. She'd gained about ten pounds since she'd split up with Thomas—mostly because she was too busy to work out or to always prepare healthy foods—but she hadn't fully restocked her wardrobe. She had decent clothes for work and casual, but these dinners with potential donors that were happening more often now were a stretch of her resources.

She had another one tonight with the same donors they'd had dinner with over the weekend—and Thomas had suggested he come stay with Mia instead of a babysitter since he wasn't on call.

Pulling out a flattering gray top with a lowish neckline and a sleek black skirt, she decided they would have to do, and she left them draped on the bed, ready to put on later. Then she headed toward the living room to make sure Mia and Thomas were all right.

She found them on the couch together with a book between them. It was an endearing sight. Thomas wore a black crew-neck shirt and beat-up tan trousers, while Mia was already dressed in her pink PJs and bunny slippers. Abigail felt a familiar clench in her heart as she saw them.

Mia was leaning against his side, and one of his arms was around her as he held the book out for both of them to see. He appeared to be trying to find the page they'd left off on.

The size of the book made Abigail blink. "What are you reading?"

"*Little Women*," Mia said happily. "We started last weekend, and we're already on chapter four!"

Abigail's eyes widened. While fairly tame, *Little Women* was definitely not written for six-year-old girls, and it included a somewhat traumatic death scene.

Thomas met her eyes blandly, raising his brows in what was almost a challenge.

She'd said he could try to find something better than the fairy school books, and he'd taken her up on it.

Abigail asked, "Are you enjoying the book, Mia?"

"Yes. It's good. Sometimes it's confusing, but Daddy explains. He says that writers today are lazy, and that people used to be able to write better."

Abigail couldn't help but chuckle, but she was genuinely concerned about how Mia would handle the much more adult second half of the book.

Mia prattled on happily. "He says that it is two books put into one and that we only get to read the first book now. I have to wait until I'm bigger to read the second book. Do you think that's right, Mommy?"

Letting out a gust of relieved laughter, Abigail said, "Yes, Daddy is right about that. You won't like the second book yet. I'm sure he'll find you something else good when you finish the first book."

She was smiling as she met Thomas's eyes, and his held clever amusement that had always been characteristic of him. Warmth filled her chest and her belly as they kept smiling at each other—completely in sync, completely understanding one another.

The feeling was so deep that Abigail actually took a step toward him, wanting to reach out and touch him.

"Oh. Okay," Mia said, blissfully ignorant of the feeling sparking in the air between her parents. She turned to peer up at Thomas's face. "Mommy's going to the symphony with Mr. Foster."

Thomas broke their shared gaze, and his eyebrows arched dramatically. "I thought it was a work function."

Abigail felt off stride by how close she'd felt to Thomas just now and then the sudden interruption. "It is a work function. We're just going with the potential donors to dinner and the symphony. Mia, Mr. Foster is there because he's my boss, but the dinner is about work. You know that."

"Okay."

Abigail wished she'd followed up on her concerns over the weekend and talked to Mia about Mr. Foster this week.

"Have you ever been to the symphony, Daddy?"

"I have."

"Did you ever take Mommy to the symphony?"

"I did." His green eyes shifted over to Abigail, and they took on a certain expression she'd almost forgotten.

Abigail sucked in her breath, feeling a flash of response to the memory he'd evoked with his look. Once again, deep feeling rushed through her, but this time it was of a different variety.

She and Thomas had gone to the symphony more than once in the years they were together, but she vividly remembered one particular time. Knew that evening was on his mind too.

Flustered and flushed, Abigail murmured, "I'm going to get ready now. Have fun reading."

As she turned on the shower and tossed her T-shirt and sweats on the floor of the bathroom, Abigail tried not to think about one particular night at the symphony—several months after they'd gotten married.

But as she stepped naked under the hot spray, she couldn't help but remember.

It was the first time she'd ever had an orgasm.

He'd splurged for expensive tickets, so they'd been sitting in an exclusive box in the theater, and Thomas had his arm around her. Just after intermission, he'd started to rub her neck and shoulders. It should have been an innocent touch, but it seemed to become more. Eventually, Abigail's body had been a lit fuse, so aroused she couldn't sit still.

Abigail had been raised to believe sex was something secret and dirty. Her parents had never actually said the words, but that conclusion had been very clear in everything they did. She'd known almost nothing about sex when she got married, and Thomas hadn't even been able to finish on their wedding night since she'd been so uncomfortable and upset.

It had been a month before they could have sex for real, and even longer before Abigail was genuinely comfortable with it.

Thomas had never been anything but careful and considerate, but he must have been so frustrated and disappointed in her. The memory of those nights and her own failures still mortified Abigail.

Because of her issues, that night in the symphony had been like a victory.

As soon as the applause erupted, Thomas had grabbed her hand and they'd fled. They'd made it to their SUV, parked in a dark corner of a parking garage.

She still remembered what it had felt like in the backseat of the SUV, fumbling around like eager teenagers. He'd brought her to climax with his hand, and then he'd pulled her over on his lap, helping her move over him. He'd been muttering out hoarse endearments, telling her how beautiful she was, how much he loved her. She hadn't come again, but the second part of their lovemaking had been just as mind-blowing to her as the first.

Recalling it now, Abigail felt her body react as well as her heart. She'd done her best not to think about sex much since the separation, but she wasn't always successful.

She forced her mind to something else, anything else as she scrubbed her hair down with shampoo, but she felt frustrated and jittery when she got out of the shower, still thinking about the look in Thomas's eyes earlier.

She wondered if he still thought about having sex with her too. Sometimes.

Glancing at the time, she realized she had to hurry now. So she dried her hair, applied careful makeup, and got dressed without dallying. When she put on her jewelry, she stared into the mirror to assess the result.

She looked perfectly nice for dinner and the symphony—and nothing like the self-conscious girl she used to be—so she grabbed her purse and headed to the living room.

"Ooh!" Mia squealed at her arrival. "Mommy looks beautiful!"

"Thank you, Mia." Abigail ran her hands down her skirt absently, feeling suddenly self-conscious at Thomas's steady gaze. His face showed no expression, but she knew he missed no detail of her appearance.

"Just in time," Thomas said, glancing at his watch. "Seven o'clock. I didn't know you took such long showers."

Abigail felt her cheeks burning, but she managed not to react in any other way. There was absolutely no way Thomas could know what she'd been thinking about in the shower. "Thanks for coming over early to sit with Mia while I got ready," she said, pleased when her voice sounded natural. "It was a huge help."

"Of course."

"I'm not sure when I'll be back, but it will be late since we're going to Dalton." She glanced outside and saw headlights turning into the driveway of her little bungalow. "That's Jim. He's picking me up, and then we'll pick up the Seymours."

"I see." Thomas's voice was strange, but she didn't know why.

"All right," Abigail said in a rush, feeling anxious and self-conscious and at loose ends. "You be good, Mia. Obey your daddy and go to bed when he says. Eight o'clock. And you can read until nine thirty."

"I know, Mommy."

"There are snacks in the kitchen," Abigail went on, looking at Thomas now. "And I'll have my phone on vibrate the whole time, so just call me any time if you need me."

"I know, Abigail," he said, his mouth twitching up a little.

"Okay." She glanced down at herself to make sure she had everything she needed. Then she told Mia, "I'll give you your good-night kiss now since you'll be asleep when I get back."

She leaned down to kiss Mia, and she was about to leave when Mia said, "You didn't give Baxter his kiss!"

Abigail hurried back over, flustered by the way Thomas's eyes never left her face. She kissed Baxter. "All right. You be good and have fun."

Then she kissed Mia again. "Mommy loves you."

"I love you, Mommy."

Rushed and thoughtless, Abigail moved to give Thomas a quick kiss on the lips in sequence. "I'll be back after midnight probably."

With a last wave, she left the living room. As she was reaching for the handle of the front door, she heard Mia's giggle rippling out from the other room.

She paused, wondering what had prompted her daughter to laugh like that.

Then Abigail realized.

She'd just kissed Thomas. On the lips. Without even thinking about it.

With a gasp, Abigail whirled around and took a few steps back, with some sort of half-formed notion to try to explain.

But she caught sight of Thomas and Mia on the couch.

Mia was shaking with merriment, her hands covering her mouth. And Thomas had one finger to his lips as he smiled at his daughter, in the universal signal to keep quiet.

Overwhelmed with confusion, Abigail fled.

It was no big deal. She'd just been in a rush and hadn't been thinking. She'd been feeling closer to him than she had in a long time. Mia obviously thought it was funny.

Maybe things were getting better. There were a lot of very positive signs.

Maybe soon kissing Thomas would be natural again.

~

Jim Foster, her boss, walked Abigail to her door when he dropped her off after midnight.

The evening had gone well. They had their spiel down to a science now, and the Seymours had been impressed and inspired to donate. Their gift would be a huge help to the estate and the projects they were hoping to begin in the house and grounds.

Jim looked very pleased as he walked her up the path, and he was laughing at something she'd said.

He was an attractive man in his early forties—divorced with no children. Abigail liked him and liked working with him.

"Thanks for driving," she said, pulling out her keys. "I'll see you on Monday morning."

"Sounds good." Jim lingered, which seemed kind of strange. Like he had something to say.

Abigail waited, having no idea what he wanted to say now that couldn't have been said at any point in the evening.

His expression changed slightly, and he seemed to move a little closer to her. She suddenly recognized the look in his eyes.

Her breath hitched, and she ducked her head, her cheeks burning in a familiar way. "Yes, well, thanks. Have a good night."

She hurriedly unlocked the door and closed it behind her, before Jim could say anything.

Surely he wasn't thinking about her romantically. That was just crazy. She wasn't single. She was still married, even if she wasn't currently living with her husband.

Plus the man was her boss.

She felt rattled and breathless and deeply confused, and she desperately hoped it was just a passing thing. She would be crushed if the career she'd been working so hard on was affected by something crazy like this.

Maybe it was just a fluke, a result of the evening, which had been set up almost like a double date. She would be careful from now on. Give him none of that kind of encouragement.

She liked to think of herself as mature and worldly now, but maybe she was still as sheltered and naïve as the girl who had married Thomas. She'd been so blind. She should have noticed this before and nipped it in the bud.

She found Thomas working on a laptop at the dining room table.

"Hi," she said, wishing the blush would fade from her cheeks. "Everything all right?"

"Yeah." Thomas closed the laptop and stood up. "Did you have a good time?"

Abigail peered at him closely and thought he looked kind of bristly. His features were a little stiff, and his shoulders were tense. "What's wrong? Is Mia all right?"

"I said," he murmured in a low voice that she recognized as suppressed impatience, "everything is fine. She turned off the light at nine thirty. She's asleep."

"Then what's wrong with you?" Giving him an annoyed look—since she'd always hated the snide tone he'd just used—she walked past him and into the kitchen, where she pulled out a glass to pour herself some filtered water from the refrigerator. She still felt too hot.

Thomas followed her. "Nothing is wrong with me. I had asked you a question you completely ignored."

Abigail thought back. "Oh. Sorry about that. I didn't mean to be rude. Yes, it was fine. I think we'll be getting a sizeable gift from them."

"And Jim Foster?"

She was leaning back against the counter, and Thomas was standing far too close to her. Once again invading her personal space. And once again his tone was snide. "What is wrong with you?"

Thomas had one hand on the counter beside her, bracing himself as he stood just a few inches away from her. His green eyes were intent on her face, and she saw his nostrils flare just a little. "You smell like him."

Abigail gasped, mostly from shock and outrage but also with the faintest trace of arousal at the intimacy of the words. "What?"

"I said," he gritted out, edging even closer until the fabric of his shirt brushed against her arm and one of her breasts, "you smell like him."

"Well, what do you expect? I spent the evening with the man."

Something grew even tenser in his expression. "Did you?"

She knew him well enough to understand the resonance in his words. "What are you thinking, Thomas?" she asked in a hushed voice, making sure her voice didn't carry past the kitchen. "What are you possibly thinking?"

Clearly Thomas too was conscious of not waking Mia since his murmur was thick, rough, and soft. "I'd like to remind you of the fact that you're still my wife."

"And you really think I need to be reminded of that?"

His lips tightened into white. "I saw him walk you to the door."

She sucked in an indignant breath and clenched her fists at her sides. Thomas was still far too close. She could feel the heat radiating off his body, sense the leashed tension in his stance, hear the fast, uneven breaths he was taking. She was angry and defensive and hurt and excited—and she felt strangely close to him—all at once. "So someone isn't allowed to be polite to me now because I'm still your wife?"

Thomas made a guttural sound and braced his other hand on the counter, imprisoning her between his arms. He leaned forward, pushing her back against the counter, and he rasped against her ear. "That man wasn't just being polite. You know it as well as I do."

She knew he was right about that. She'd been foolish in not recognizing what Jim was thinking long before now. But he didn't have to act like he thought she would actually respond to it.

Beneath her tumultuous emotions was a familiar feeling building beneath her belly. She knew how to recognize it. Knew it was triggered by the proximity of Thomas's lean, hard body, his familiar scent flooding her senses, his piercing eyes and thick voice.

She wanted him so much. She'd never stopped wanting him. No matter what happened between them.

"Why are you acting this way?" She stiffened her back and tried to ease her groin away from Thomas's hip since she was fighting the temptation to grind herself against it.

Thomas seemed to suddenly pull himself together, and he jerked away from her. He turned around so his back was toward her, and she saw him take a few long breaths.

Abigail was trembling helplessly.

When he turned around, he seemed to have gotten himself under control. His forehead was damp and his back was still stiff, but his hands were relaxed at his side. He spoke in his natural voice. "You have to acknowledge that right now it is my concern whether or not you date other men."

"Of course it is. But I'm not dating Jim. How can you think that? He's my boss. You and I have been doing really well lately. I mean, I've thought things were going well. Surely you trust me enough to know I'm not going to date other men." She paused, swallowing hard. "Don't you?"

He let out a thick breath. "Of course I do."

"Okay."

They stood in the kitchen awkwardly. Abigail shifted from foot to foot, wishing she could hug him. Or something.

But things still felt too uncertain between them, and they were supposed to be on their break.

"I'll get going," Thomas said at last.

They both went back into the living room, where Thomas slid his laptop into his case.

"Don't forget Mia's going to be staying at your parents' tomorrow," Abigail said, trying to summon back their normal interaction. "Since I have to be at Milbourne House all day and you're at work."

"Yeah," he said, straightening up and looking deeply exhausted, kind of the way she felt. "I remember. Hope tomorrow goes well for you."

She knew his last comment and the quirk of a smile that went with it was a kind of peace offering. She returned his smile sincerely before they said good night.

Although she was glad they'd basically come to terms, she was still shaky and overly emotional when she closed and locked the door.

She peeked into Mia's room to make sure the girl was still sleeping. When that was confirmed, she went to get ready for bed.

It wasn't long before she crawled under the covers, but she didn't feel sleepy.

She felt wired.

Arguing with Thomas had always done this to her—left her feeling jittery and at loose ends.

Abigail found herself remembering one occasion, on their third anniversary, when they'd come home after what was supposed to be a romantic evening.

They'd seen one of the nurses at the hospital when they'd stopped in a bakery for dessert, and that was what had prompted the fight.

The nurse was obviously close to Thomas—they spent a lot of time together at the hospital—and Abigail had been horribly jealous of the gorgeous, sexy brunette who could have been a model and who made her feel like a dumpy, dowdy plebian.

"You're being ridiculous," Thomas had snapped, as he closed their bedroom door to make sure their voices didn't carry to where two-year-old Mia was sleeping down the hall. "You can't possibly think I'm having an affair with her."

"That's not the point! You know how it makes me feel when you have all these beautiful female friends, and yet you still hang out with them all the time."

"That's where I work. I can't help but hang around with them. Besides, I can't always dance around your insecurities. You need to learn to trust me."

"This isn't about trust. It's about your surrounding yourself with gorgeous women. How do you think that makes me feel?"

Thomas had been shaking with frustration. "You're my wife. I love you. I married you. *That's* how I expect you to feel!"

They'd been arguing for more than a half hour—all the way home from the bakery—and the fight had basically run its course. Thomas's words were the last straw for Abigail. She'd thrown herself on him with urgent passion, clutching at his head as she kissed him, grinding her body against his.

He'd responded immediately, lifting her by the hips until she wrapped her legs around him and then carrying her over to the bed. She wouldn't release him, even after he eased her down, and they didn't take the time to remove their clothes. Thomas just unfastened his pants and Abigail pushed up her skirt.

They rutted like animals, Thomas half off the bed and Abigail beneath him. They grunted and panted and shook the bed hard.

Shaking and sweating, Abigail had still wanted more. "Harder. I need it harder." He'd given her a pendant necklace for their anniversary, and she had felt the weight of it against her throat.

Thomas had pushed into her fiercely, forcing her body backward on each thrust. "Tell me you trust me," he'd rasped.

"I trust you."

Thomas thrust hard.

Her head tossing restlessly, she gasped it out again. "I trust you."

Another powerful thrust.

"I trust you."

They kept it up until they both reached climax.

Remembering that evening, Abigail's body pulsed with arousal, but a few tears burned in her eyes as she tried to process the memory.

And there was one truth she kept going back to, feeling like she was seeing it—seeing herself—anew for the first time.

When she'd told Thomas she trusted him over and over again that evening so long ago, she hadn't entirely believed it.

~

It was after nine o'clock on Saturday evening when Abigail returned from working the function at Milbourne House.

Everything had gone fine, but now she was tired and didn't feel much like doing anything.

Mia was still with Thomas's parents. It was after bedtime now, so Abigail would go pick her up first thing in the morning. She should probably try to go to bed early and catch up on her sleep, but Abigail felt restless and bored.

And a little lonely.

The small house seemed vast and empty without Mia's presence. Abigail changed into a tank and a pair of yoga pants and decided she might as well be a coach potato all evening. She called to get an update on how Mia was doing. Then she flipped on the television.

A knock at the door startled her.

Jumping to her feet, she went to peer out the peephole.

Saw Thomas.

She swung open the door. "Hi," she said, feeling a jump of pleasure in her heart at the sight of him.

"Hi." He smiled at her ruefully. He was dressed fairly casually in a crew-neck shirt and gray trousers. "How was the thing today?"

"Fine. I thought you were working."

"I just got off."

"Oh." Then she noticed he was holding something behind his back. "What's that?"

With an almost sheepish expression, Thomas showed her a bottle of wine. "That is an apology."

Abigail looked from the wine to Thomas's face and back again. It was Merlot. Her favorite kind. She was so overwhelmed she couldn't think for a moment.

He shifted slightly at her hesitation. "I'm assuming it's still your favorite. I feel bad about last night."

She met his eyes and recognized that he looked slightly embarrassed.

She smiled, affection flooding her cheeks and rising to her throat. The understated gesture was so much like Thomas, and there was no one in the world like him.

"Thank you. I don't have anything to do this evening. If you want, you can come in and we'll open the bottle."

∼

Abigail was laughing so hard she could barely speak. The living room was warm and just a little blurred at the edges, and she couldn't remember the last time she'd felt so relaxed.

Choking on her hilarity, she managed to finish her story. "And then... and then she looked up at that crass teenager through her little glasses and said... and said he should be ashamed of himself. Whistling at ladies was rude and dem... demean..." Abigail had to gasp for air between her cackles before she finished. "Demeaning!"

Thomas laughed with her, more warmly and openly than she'd seen him laugh in a long time. "I wish I'd been there."

"You should have been there. It was the funniest thing."

They were both slouched on the couch, and they'd finished the wine he'd brought over.

"Whew! I think I'm buzzed."

"You never did have much tolerance."

"You don't have to make it sound like it's a flaw in my design." Feeling overly warm, she pulled the fabric of her tank top away from her chest and tried to blow some air down her neckline. Then her eyes widened dramatically. "I don't have a bra on."

"I noticed that."

"Why didn't you tell me?"

He gave a matter-of-fact shrug. "Doesn't bother me. I've seen the parts in question before."

Abigail huffed for a minute, until she decided on the reasonableness of his claims. But just to make sure they were on an equal playing field, she said with what she thought was impressive acumen, "I've seen your parts too. Don't forget."

"I haven't forgotten. You were always very good to my parts."

Even through the pleasant blur the world had become, Abigail recognized something off about his words. She sat up straight and gasped. "You're buzzed too!"

"Nope."

"You are! How much wine did you drink?"

"Not much. You drank most of it."

"I did not. I drank…" She paused, trying to recall the number of glasses she'd drunk. Neither one of them were big drinkers, but her tolerance was particularly low. Finally, she gave up on figuring it out. She slumped back in a happy daze and turned her head to stare at Thomas.

He looked overly warm too. His face was slightly flushed, and there was a sheen of perspiration on his skin. As she watched, he took the bottom of his shirt and lifted it to casually wipe some of the sweat off his face. The move bared a flat, toned belly. One she'd always found irresistible.

She reached over to poke it.

Thomas grunted.

She poked his belly again.

He grunted.

He caught her hand before she could poke him one more time.

"Hey!" she said reproachfully.

"Hands to yourself."

"Hmph. You used to like my hands on you." She tried to glare at him but couldn't quite coordinate the expression.

"You used to like my hands on you."

"Oh." It was an excellent point. She couldn't think of an appropriate rejoinder.

So she gave a long sigh and concluded, "I'm buzzed."

"You said that before."

She wrinkled her nose and prepared to give him a good setdown. Then she noticed how incredibly gorgeous he looked, sprawled and rumpled on the couch beside her.

And she got a better idea. He must have always thought she was uptight and unsexy, so she would prove him otherwise. She crawled across the length of the couch and plopped down in his lap. "Maybe we can be buzzed together," she said, stroking his head with eager fingers.

Thomas exhaled slowly, thickly, and his hands settled on the curve of her bottom. "Don't see why not."

Abigail's head was spinning, and a giddy flush warmed her skin. Conscious of nothing but the sudden urge to touch, she leaned forward toward his attractive, so-familiar face.

Her lips landed, not on his mouth, but on his chin.

Undeterred by her poor aim, she pressed a series of wet kisses in a line along his jaw. "Being buzzed is fun," she mumbled as she mouthed her way up to his ear.

"Mm-hmm," Thomas agreed, one of his hands still squeezing her ass and the other edging up toward her chest.

She sucked on his earlobe vigorously, closing her eyes as Thomas palmed one of her breasts. Humming in pleasure, she finally released his lobe and stuck her tongue in his ear.

He grunted.

Delighted by this reaction, she tried the move again, this time fluttering her tongue while she rubbed her fingers over his scalp.

Thomas grunted again, and his tense body gave a little twitch.

Abigail felt an arousal pulsing between her legs, but she couldn't identify exactly what had triggered it or when she'd become aware of it. With fuzzy satisfaction, she kept tonguing Thomas's ear and caressing the back of his neck, which she remembered had always been particularly sensitive.

She sensed his body growing tighter and tighter beneath her, and he huffed out guttural, uncontrolled sounds that thrilled her. Even before things had fallen apart, he'd always seemed so careful and controlled.

But she knew she was turning him on at the moment, and her blurred thought process understood this as reason enough to keep doing it.

Eventually, her tongue got tired, so she moistened her lips and then rubbed them along his temple. When he moaned softly, she asked, "You like that?"

"Mm," he hummed. He'd been doing his best to fondle her breasts through her tank top, hampered by her awkward position above him on the couch.

"You're not saying much," she complained, feeling like she was doing all the work in sustaining the conversation.

Still straddling his lap, she raised herself higher on her knees so she could run her lips across his forehead.

"Otherwise occupied," Thomas murmured, taking advantage of her higher position to pull one of her breasts out of the neckline of her top.

Abigail was briefly peeved that he sounded slightly more articulate than her, but that mild irritation vanished when he closed his lips around her nipple. He suckled with more enthusiasm than skill, but the stimulation caused her intimate muscles to clench.

She reached down and discovered he was hard in his pants. She did her best to massage him, rewarded when he groaned softly.

Then suddenly he was lifting her off his lap, putting her down on the couch beside him. It was like something had changed in him, clicked in him, turned off.

Or maybe on.

"What's going on?" She started to move over him again, her body desperately craving what only he could give her. "I wanted to—"

"I know, baby," he murmured, gently moving her hand from his groin. "I'm sorry. But not like this. Not when you're buzzed."

Her face twisted in frustration. "I want to. I wouldn't do it if I wasn't buzzed."

"I know," he said again, grabbing her wrists so she couldn't reach for his erection again. "That's why we have to stop."

There was something final in his tone that even her fuzzy mind could recognize. So she slumped down against him, disappointed, frustrated, and heavy with something even deeper. "I wanted to," she murmured.

He wrapped an arm around her. "I know. I did too." He sighed. "Shit, I drank too much."

"Is the room spinning for you?"

"Nope."

She huffed. "Party pooper." Then when a wave of dizziness hit her, she said, "Oh."

"Tell me if you're gonna be sick."

"Nope." She grinned up at him, pleased that she'd thought of such a witty retort.

"Nope—you won't tell me? Or nope—you won't be sick?"

"Nope, won't tell you and won't be sick," she said with more confidence than was entirely warranted.

With an uneven laugh, Thomas tightened his arm.

Abigail sighed, rubbing her cheek against his shirt. "You feel nice."

"You think so?"

"I do. I've always loved how you feel."

"You feel nice too." He tilted his head down and nuzzled her hair.

She didn't see anything wrong with that. She felt like nuzzling too. So she nuzzled his shirt since it was the only thing she could reach in her present position. "I do?"

"Mm-hmm," he murmured, blowing her hair with his breath. "Soft and warm and..."

"And what?"

"Abigail-like."

That sounded perfectly reasonable to her so she smiled against his shirt.

She turned a little, vaguely looking toward his face, although she couldn't really focus on it. "You okay?"

"I'm good."

"Good," she sighed. Her head still spinning, she nestled against him and closed her eyes.

The world went dark before she could process anything else.

~

When Abigail woke up, her head pounded and her mouth felt like it was filled with foul-tasting cotton.

She edged her eyes open just slightly and smacked her lips a few times. "Oh God," she groaned as she realized how bad she felt.

With some effort, she managed to sit up, although her head hurt so much she squeezed her forehead with one hand. She looked down at herself to find she still wore her yoga pants and tank top from last night.

And suddenly she knew why. A flood of knowledge hit her like a wave.

"Oh God," she groaned again as the previous night came back to her.

"That bad?"

She gasped at the male voice from her doorway. Thomas stood, fully dressed and relatively presentable, in the clothes he'd worn last night. He must have already showered since he looked fully awake. There were dark circles under his eyes, however. He held two glasses of water.

She reached out for one as she tried to think of something to say. A glance beside her revealed that the other side of the bed had been slept in. Her eyes shot over to Thomas. "What... what happened?"

He sat cautiously on the edge of the bed beside her. "You don't remember?"

"I remember... Oh no. Fumbling around on the couch, groping and... Oh no!" Blazing with mortification, she fell back in the bed again. "Is that all we did?"

"Yes. That's all."

"Did I pass out?"

"I think you just fell asleep. I carried you to bed."

Abigail looked over at the opposite side of her bed. "You slept over?"

Thomas's face was very still, very careful. "I did. I wasn't in any shape to go home. I hope that's all right."

"Yeah. Of course." She rubbed her face and groaned a little more. Then she found the initiative to sit up again and drink some water.

"I'm making coffee," Thomas told her, his eyes scanning her face closely.

"Thanks."

She groaned, remembering how shamelessly she'd been pawing at him last night. "I can't believe I did that. I'll never live this down."

Her father had always been impatient of any sort of weakness, any sort of foolishness. He'd believed human nature needed to be rigorously kept under control. She no longer believed the same things her father had about that, but it was hard to kick the feeling of never being good enough.

Of shame. At being weak. At being foolish. At doing things a good girl would never do.

"I'm the only other person who was there," Thomas said softly.

That was true. There was a kind of safety in that, in only his knowing her foolishness. More than once during their marriage, Thomas had left her feeling not good enough too, but he wasn't acting like that now. He didn't look like he was judging her, resenting her.

He'd changed. She had too.

This wasn't the end of the world.

She smiled at him shakily. "Thank you."

"For what?" He looked genuinely confused.

"For stopping us. I appreciate it. I remember enough to know what happened."

"I'm sorry I let it go as far as it did." He rubbed a hand over his face.

"Well, if truth be told, you were a little buzzed too." Before he could object or reply, she added, "Okay. No big deal really. We drank too much. These things happen."

"Yeah."

"Good." She groaned one more time as it felt like someone was taking a hammer to her head. "Shoot. It's after eight. Mia. I've got to go get her."

"Let me drive you," Thomas said. Before she could object, he said, "I've got to get to the hospital anyway, and you're in no shape to drive this morning. I'll drop you all back and then head to work."

"Thanks," she said, holding onto her head but feeling another wave of appreciation for Thomas's consideration. He'd never been particularly romantic, but he'd always seemed to think of little things and take care of them for her. "Did you say there was coffee?"

Abigail relaxed against the passenger seat of Thomas's car.

Her headache had eased some, and now she just felt bone tired and kind of achy about last night.

She wished she hadn't been so silly, but it wasn't as bad as it felt. It was embarrassing. And it would have been nice if it had never happened.

But it seemed like it wasn't going to change the positive progress that had happened between them.

They still had a few months before they had to jump back into all the struggle and angst of really working on their marriage. If things kept going the way they were, maybe both of them would have grown and changed enough for them to finally settle everything that was wrong.

Praying silently over their marriage, Abigail sipped her coffee and looked out the window. They were stopped at a red light, about to turn onto the highway, which was the closest way to get to the other side of town where Thomas's parents lived.

The light turned green, and Thomas started off.

An unspecified noise caused Abigail to look across the intersection. She stared in a blurred haze at an approaching vehicle.

A vehicle approaching way too fast.

Her final thought was that the pickup truck would never be able to stop in time to brake for the red light.

The pickup didn't stop at all.

It just crashed into the passenger side of Thomas's car, in a deafening impact of noise, metal, and glass.

THREE

Please be okay. Please be okay. Please be okay.

She heard the words, the vaguely familiar voice, coming out of the darkness.

And then somehow she was saying them, knocking on the door to Thomas's study, a small finished porch off the back of their rented house in Durham. It was only seven months after they'd gotten married, and she was muttering under her breath, "Please be okay. Please be okay with it."

She was so nervous her hands were shaking, but she steeled her will and knocked louder when her first faint tap got no response.

He'd been at the hospital for nearly twenty hours straight, and he'd gone right to his study when he got home.

She understood that his surgical residency program was high stress and incredibly hard work, even more so now than it had been when she'd first met him, but it felt like days went by without her ever seeing him. And she hated the feeling of being afraid to interrupt her own husband.

Her father had been that way. He'd be reading the Bible or doing devotions, and she and her mom were never allowed to bother him.

She'd sworn her own family wasn't going to be like that.

But here she was. Knocking on the closed door. Absolutely terrified.

When he called out a monosyllabic response, she opened the door and stuck her head in. "Hey. Do you have a minute?"

Thomas looked up at her from the book he was pouring over and smiled. He looked tired and a little distracted, and stress was evident in his eyes, in the lines on his forehead.

When they'd first gotten married, she'd been determined to help him really relax when he was home, but she'd given up on that fairy tale eventually. He simply wouldn't relax.

"Hi," he said, leaning back in his chair and rubbing a hand over his brown hair. "Is everything all right?"

"Yeah. I just needed to talk to you for a few minutes."

"Sure." Thomas glanced back at his book. "Give me five minutes, and I'll be done in here."

Abigail let out her held breath and ducked out of the study. Restless and anxious, she paced the hall and then wandered into the one bathroom in the two-bedroom house.

There she picked up the plastic stick from the home pregnancy kit she'd been staring at for the past hour. "Please be okay. Please be okay. Please be okay with it," she murmured, closing her eyes as a new wave of fear washed over her.

They hadn't been married for very long. She was still working on her master's, and Thomas wasn't anywhere close to finishing his residency. They'd talked about kids before they got married and agreed they would wait until they were settled.

This wasn't supposed to have happened.

She was praying silently, desperately, her eyes closed, when she heard his voice in the hall and came out to meet him, holding the little stick behind her back.

"Are you all right?" Thomas asked, eyeing her with a quiet scrutiny that was very familiar. "You look a little shaky."

Sometimes she wondered what he was thinking, what secret flaws and failures he thought he would find when he peered at her with such intent observation.

"I'm all right." Her voice cracked on the last word.

His brows drew together, and he glanced back at the bathroom. "Are you sick again? If you are, I'm calling the doctor. No arguments this time. You shouldn't have gone to class or Bible study this week."

"I enjoy Bible study." She'd only begun a new women's Bible study a month ago, but she felt closer to God than she ever had before, for the first time understanding how grace meant she didn't always have to try to be good enough. The study felt like a revelation to her, and she didn't want to miss a single week. "And I have to go to class if I want to pass."

"Yeah, but you don't really need to pass, do you? It's just something you're doing to kill time, so what does it matter? If you're sick, then you should stay home and get better."

She started to object. She'd started the degree primarily for something to do outside her mostly empty home, but she'd begun to enjoy her coursework and was invested now in the degree—something he should know since she'd told him all about it quite often this semester—so it bothered her that he kept referring to it like a hobby that had no real significance.

But this was hardly the time to get into an argument.

"I'm not sick," she said instead, taking a breath and steeling her will again. "But I will need to see a doctor."

She handed him the plastic stick with a slightly trembling hand.

Thomas took the stick and stared down at it. He didn't move. Didn't speak. Just appeared frozen for a long time. For far too long.

Abigail gulped over the lump in her throat. "The little plus means yes."

"Wha—?" Finally breaking out of his stupor, Thomas cut off the word and shook his head hard. "I don't—"

"I've been good about the birth control," she said in a rush, with a surge of fear that he'd assume she'd done it on purpose. "I must just be in that small percentage that gets pregnant anyway."

Thomas opened his mouth but no sound came out. His gaze shifted from the stick to Abigail's face.

"I know we didn't plan this," Abigail said, her voice breaking a few times. She put a hand on her belly. "But... our baby. Are you... are you okay?"

He walked into the bedroom and sat down on the edge of the bed abruptly. "Yes. Yes, of course, I'm okay. I'm just surprised."

Abigail hugged her arms to her middle, following him and shaking even more now than before. "Are you sure?" she whispered. "I know we were going to wait until you were done with your residency and everything, but I want you to be happy."

"Of course I'm happy," Thomas said, his voice soothing now and natural. He held out his arms. "Come here, baby. Of course I'm happy."

She went to him, let him gather her into his lap, hold her in a tight embrace, and murmur out reassurances.

After a few minutes, her shaking stopped. And soon they were able to talk about it, make plans for the future.

Abigail didn't leave the security of Thomas's arms for a long time, but she also didn't look too deeply into his eyes.

She was too afraid of what she might see there.

~

Please be okay. Please be okay. Please be okay.

Like before, she heard the voice through the darkness until it morphed into words she was saying herself as she once again knocked on the door to Thomas's study in Durham. This time, four years had gone by, but she was once again muttering under her breath, "Please be okay. Please be okay with it."

She didn't hear a response, but she didn't wait for one. She just opened the door. It was a room in her house. She was allowed to enter without permission.

Thomas blinked up at her from the book he'd been pouring over. He still spent most of his downtime from the hospital studying. "What?"

"I wanted to talk to you if that's allowed." Her tone might have been a little snippy, but she was so, so tired of waiting for spare moments to talk to her own husband. Over the years, it had just gotten worse.

"About what?"

"I was looking around at jobs," she began, going into her prepared speech.

"For me?" he said, interrupting.

She stiffened in annoyance. "For *me*."

This seemed to get his attention. He put down his book and straightened his shoulders. "Why are you looking for a job?"

"Why shouldn't I look for a job? I've got two master's degrees now, and I've done exactly nothing with them. Why shouldn't I look around and see if there's something I'd be good at, work that could make me happy."

Something went cold on his face. She saw it happen the way she'd seen it happen dozens of times before—whenever she tried to talk to him about how she'd changed, matured, grown out of the insecure girl he had married. "We don't know where we'll be next year."

"I know that, but it can't hurt to look around. There aren't that many jobs I can do that use my degrees." She cleared her throat, her heart dropping heavily as she saw nothing of kindness or understanding in his expression. "It's not like I have to work, but I don't see why I shouldn't look around just in case it works out. Anyway, I found this. It looks perfect for us."

She handed him the job ad she'd printed off and had been praying over for a week now.

He accepted the wrinkled page on the open position at Milbourne House in the mountains of North Carolina and stared down at it for far longer than it would take him to read.

Finally, she couldn't stand it any longer. "That's near Willow Park," she said.

"I see that." He still hadn't looked up from the page.

"We always talked about moving back to that area since your family is there and everything, so I noticed it right away. You could easily get a job at a hospital nearby, so I thought it might be worth… worth looking into. Just to consider."

He wasn't happy. She could tell he wasn't happy from the lines of his face, the posture of his shoulders, the tension in the air.

He wasn't happy at all.

"What about Mia?" he asked, finally looking up to meet her eyes.

"What *about* Mia?"

"You're planning to take this job and just leave her—"

"I'm thinking of getting a job—not abandoning our child on the street. Why shouldn't I considering getting a job I'd be good at, one I'd enjoy?" She felt sick and put a hand on her belly. She was angry and terrified and hurt and betrayed and uncertain, the conflicting feelings all tightening into a hard knot.

"Of course you can consider getting a job," Thomas said at last, the tension on his face relaxing but not into anything like peace or acceptance. It was that cool, superior irony she disliked more than any of his other expressions. "You know perfectly well I'm okay with that. But it seems like the priority should be our family—and not some fantasy job to fulfill your own personal dreams. So maybe you should just hold off and see where we end up and then start looking for a job that works out with our whole situation."

She stared at him, experiencing a hot and familiar wave of shame. He thought she was being selfish—thinking of herself at the expense of their family. And maybe he was right.

She'd spent most of her life assuming she wouldn't work outside the home. It was the lifestyle she'd been raised to believe was the only one appropriate for women. She'd started changing after she'd first joined that Bible study, and she no longer believed what she used to. But maybe she'd taken it too far. Maybe she had somehow become selfish. She knew so many women who prayed for the day they could stay at home with their children. And here she was…

"Okay?" Thomas prompted, with a lift of his eyebrows.

She nodded, swallowing hard, feeling the way she always had as a child when her father gave her a sermon, telling her how God expected her to be a better girl. She picked up the paper and crumpled it with her hand. She murmured, "Okay. That makes sense."

∽

Abigail, wake up. Abigail, baby, wake up.

The voice was coming out of the darkness again, and this time it was paired with a soft shake of her shoulder. "Abigail, wake up."

Four months had passed since that conversation in the study about the job, and Thomas was now trying to wake her up.

Abigail groaned reluctantly, attempting to turn away from the intrusive presence.

"I'm sorry, Abigail, but you need to wake up." The grip on her shoulder tightened slightly and the shaking grew more forceful.

"Too early," she mumbled, trying to keep her eyes closed.

"I know it's early, but I have to leave."

And that jarred away the last remnants of sleep. Her eyes popped open, and she was confronted with a vision of Thomas—fully dressed in a suit and tie—sitting on the edge of their bed and looking down at her. "What? *What?*"

"My plane leaves in a couple of hours."

"But," she croaked, forcing her foggy mind to work. "I thought you weren't going."

"I said I'd think about it. But it's too good an opportunity not to consider. I'm not saying I'll take it, but I have to at least give it a chance. It would make my entire career."

Of course it would. Thomas was brilliant, and he had almost completed his residency program at Duke. Hospitals and medical groups were falling all over themselves to get him. But this particular opportunity meant moving halfway across the country and taking a high-stress job that guaranteed she and Mia would hardly ever see him.

"But we were going to stay in North Carolina." Abigail was becoming more and more aware of what was happening now, and a heavy weight of dread started sinking in her gut. "It was all working out. Being close to our families, a low-stress position for you so you could be around more, the job for me…"

She'd applied for the job at Milbourne House after all a few weeks after she'd agreed to wait and see since the position was closing and she would have lost her chance completely. She'd talked to Thomas about it, and he hadn't looked happy but he hadn't objected.

Last week, she'd gotten the job offer.

"I know that," Thomas said coolly, looking slightly annoyed by the reproach. "I'm not saying that won't work out. But my job is more important than…" He trailed off before he finished the thought, but she knew exactly what he'd been going to say. "I just need to give this a chance before I make a decision."

"But—"

"I have to go, Abigail."

Anger spiraled up, momentarily overwhelming the doomed burden of acknowledgment underlying it. "So you're going to decide on your own? What's best for our family? You're just going to decide on your own?"

"Abigail, please," he said curtly, standing up, the release of his weight causing the mattress to shift. "Don't be unreasonable. You know I hate when you're emotional like this."

Her first response was to hold her tongue, rein in her angry and crushing disappointment. And then she was furious with herself for that instinctive response, as if she'd been trained to always cave without question to a man's will. "Unreasonable? Emotional? I'm so sorry my feelings bother you so much."

"Don't be sarcastic."

"I will be sarcastic if you're going to be so—"

He didn't give her the chance to even finish the sentence. "I have to leave. I'll give you a call when the plane lands. Give Mia a kiss for me."

And then he just turned around and walked for the door.

"Don't leave, Thomas," she called after him, her voice almost a plea. "Please don't leave me."

Thomas closed the door quietly behind him, and the sound seemed to signal his final answer, the nature of their marriage, their entire future.

Don't leave me. Baby, please don't leave me.

~

I can't do this without you. I really can't do this without you.

The words were still coming from outside her and then turning into something she said. This time it was during the last of the marriage counseling sessions they'd done before Christmas.

Since they'd both quickly fallen into angry accusations today, Lorraine, the counselor, asked them to start using "I" statements.

"I understand what you're saying," Abigail said slowly, working hard to keep her emotions under control. "But I can't do this without you. I know I was always too jealous and insecure, and I know it wasn't fair of me to blame you for it. But it's one part of the whole picture of our relationship, so it's not something I can work through on my own. I can't fix this without you."

"Am I asking you to fix it on your own?" Thomas's shoulders were stiff, and his face was unrevealing—sure signs that he was upset and defensive.

Lorraine lifted her eyebrows, but before she could say anything, Thomas rephrased, "I don't understand why you think I've expected you to fix it on your own. I'm here twice a week to work through this with you."

Abigail thought for a minute so she could say what came next in the clearest way possible, her hands twisting in her lap. "I know you're here. I really appreciate it. I know you want to work through this as much as I do. But every time I try to explain how I feel or what wasn't working for me, I don't feel like you've really heard me."

"Of course I've heard you." Thomas's voice was soft and rough, and his expression twisted slightly with impatience. "I've heard it over and over again for more than a year now. How many times do we have to go over it?"

The words—his clear frustration with her and the implication that she was the only one with the real problem—hurt so much she froze, focused down on her clenched hands.

Lorraine said gently, "Okay. Maybe you can explain to Abigail what it is you've heard from her about your marriage."

Thomas took a ragged breath and shifted in the upholstered chair. "You left me because…" When Lorraine cleared her throat, he stopped and began again. "I understand that you left because you wanted more than you had."

This was so unexpected—and so completely wrong—that Abigail stared at her husband. "I wanted more than I had?"

He'd been meeting her eyes, but now he looked away. "You wanted to work. You wanted this job. You wanted me to spend more time with Mia. You wanted more independence. I understand that. And I keep telling you that I'm okay with it." His voice thickened with the last words, matching the tightly repressed feeling in his face.

"But you're angry," she began. Then remembered the "I" statements. "I feel like you're angry about it—even now. Like you're just going to put up with me so you can have a wife back, but it's not really me you want."

Thomas released a brief sound of frustration and rubbed his face. "I don't care if you work. You never wanted to before we got married, but I don't *care*. I'm not your father, and I'm really tired of you assuming I'm just as narrow-minded as he is."

Abigail was again consumed with the reality that he wasn't hearing her at all. He didn't understand her at all. He thought all this was just about her job and the time he spent with Mia.

He really believed that was their whole problem.

A tight shuddering had begun inside her, slowly spreading out through her body.

"Abigail?" Lorraine prompted. "Did you want to respond?"

She took several breaths before she spoke. "I know you're not my father. The main issue isn't even my job. That's just a symptom of something deeper. And I still feel like you have no idea what the deeper thing is, no matter how many times I've tried to tell you."

Thomas held her eyes, looking tense and overly controlled—almost stoic. "Then tell me again."

Abigail made herself say it. "I feel like you see me only as a wife and not as a whole person, so you're never happy when I'm not the wife you always wanted."

"What the hell—" Thomas cut off his initial reaction, controlling himself even before Lorraine broke in. He visibly calmed down before he continued, "I don't see how you can possibly say that, after everything I've done for you."

Abigail just stared at him, her heart aching in her chest.

When she didn't respond, Thomas went on, "I don't see how you can possibly believe that. I moved here because of you. I gave up my career because of you. I sacrificed everything because you wanted me to—because you didn't think you had enough. What else do you want me to give up for you? Exactly how much do you want me to suffer until you think I've suffered enough?"

He'd slowly lost his grip on his emotions as he was speaking, and she knew the words pouring out now were the absolute expression of his heart.

He believed it. He believed that she had no genuine reason to be discontent—that their marriage had been mostly fine and that she was blowing little things out of proportion.

The truth of it hit her so hard she was blinded, choked by it. She hugged her arms to her chest to try to hold the emotion in.

He thought she was making him jump through a series of hoops and he should now be rewarded for accomplishing them.

"You..." She cleared her throat as the words strangled in her throat. "You really think that about me?"

"We both know very well that it's true."

His voice was hard and cold, but her vision was blurred so she couldn't see his face.

"Okay," she managed to say, staring down at her hands. "Okay. That's really what you believe. I'm the problem. You've done nothing wrong, and the problem really is that I'm not good enough. I'm selfish, irrational, and demanding."

"I'm not saying that. I know I made mistakes before, but I've fixed them. I've *fixed* them. And now there's nothing else I can do."

She lifted her head to see him, and they might as well have been strangers.

He didn't know her at all—he didn't understand any of what she'd gone through over the past six years, all the ways she'd grown to understand herself more, to understand God's love more, to understand that life was more than constantly striving to clean herself up.

He didn't believe he could do anything better than he was doing right now. He didn't know how much she was hurting. He thought she was just making a fuss over nothing.

Even as she heard Lorraine breaking in, telling Thomas that he should try to listen to what he'd just said, how it implied a marriage was nothing more than a series of tasks to perform, Abigail was suddenly so exhausted that she wasn't sure how she could take the next breath.

They'd been in counseling for what felt like ages, and they clearly weren't any further along than they'd been at the beginning.

It was never going to be over, never going to get better, never going to get to a place where they didn't have to desperately struggle for every step forward they took.

He was never going to really hear her, and she was never going to be able to be who he wanted.

Thomas sat just a few feet away from her, but it felt like there were vast endless miles between them.

Then there were more words out of the darkness, coming from even farther away. Words she'd never heard before.

I'm right here. Baby, I'm right here beside you. I'm not going anywhere. Please come back to me.

FOUR

Instead of the muffled, echoing voices of before, voices from the past, Abigail heard only silence.

She was conscious of a fierce pounding of her head, and she saw nothing but blackness.

For a long stretch of time, this frightened her. The world had turned dark, silent, and unrevealing. But gradually she thought of something she might be able to do about it.

Very slowly, very carefully, she edged open her eyes.

The sterile light of the room hit her vision and caused a jolt of pain to shoot through her head. With a gasp, she squeezed her eyes shut again.

"Abigail?" The thick voice was soft, male, and familiar. It was clearly in the room now, not echoing through her head like before. But she'd never—not once—heard his voice sound like this. "Abigail, baby, are you there?"

He sounded so anguished she couldn't bear not to answer. "Maybe," she croaked, the one word ripping through her dry throat.

She heard another noise. It still seemed to come from his presence, but this one she definitely couldn't identify. It was utterly foreign to everything she'd ever understood about him. It sounded choked, stifled, guttural. Broken.

But it confused and intrigued her enough for her to try to lift her eyelids again. She managed just the slightest crack, her eyelashes shading the worst of the light. This time, it didn't hurt quite so much, so she raised them a little farther.

Thomas sat in a chair beside her. His face was pale and damp, as if he'd been perspiring, but his expression was composed, just slightly strained.

"What happened?" She forced herself to shift her eyes around her, and she discovered she was in a hospital room. As instinct caught up to her before anything else, she gasped. "Mia?"

"Mia is fine. We were in a car accident," Thomas said softly. "You took a significant blow to the head. You might not remember the accident. That's normal."

She tried to think back, recall anything about being in car accident, but it hurt too much to make her mind work that way. As awareness continued to come back to her, she was suddenly conscious of the way her whole body hurt.

She glanced down and saw bindings on her arm.

"You broke a bone in your arm," Thomas explained. "And cracked a couple of ribs."

"Oh." She swallowed. When she was able to get her eyes focused on Thomas once more, something about his expression made her heart pound in fear.

He looked perfectly calm, perfectly stoic. But she saw some sort of pained emotion shuddering under the surface of his absolute composure.

"Am I..." She cleared her voice. "Am I all right?"

"Yes. Broken bones and some bruises. The hit on the head was the most serious thing."

Despite his words, she knew it wasn't that simple. Her hands started to shake under the blanket. "Am I... Am I disfigured or something?"

"No. You have some bruising and broken skin, but all of it will heal." His mouth twisted slightly. "Does it feel like you're disfigured?"

"No, but something is wrong. Why do you look like I'm dying?"

Thomas took a deep breath and exhaled it hoarsely. "You've been unconscious since the accident. We assumed it was a severe concussion and you'd shortly become conscious again." He swallowed so hard she could see it in his throat. "You were unconscious for almost three hours. That's a really long time for a concussion. I've been waiting for you to wake up."

And then Abigail understood. Thomas had been worried about her. Worried that she'd slip into a coma or even worse. That was why he looked so stiff and guarded.

The wave of emotion she experienced at this realization was almost more than she could handle in her current state.

"I think I'm all right." She tried moving her arms and legs very slightly. Everything moved. It just hurt like hell, and she was on the verge of bursting into tears.

Thomas took another shaky breath and then asked, "What's the last thing you remember?"

"I remember last night. You and me..." Despite everything, her cheeks burned with embarrassment. "And we talked this morning—I remember that. You said—" She gasped. "Oh no! You were driving! Are you okay?"

"I'm fine. Shaken up a little but not injured. You bore the brunt of the impact."

She relaxed in relief, realizing how devastated she'd be if something had happened to Thomas. The thought was troubling, and it made her think about something else. "Mia? Where is she? You said she was fine."

"She is fine. She's still at my parents'. I didn't want her to come see you until you'd woken up."

"Did you talk to her?"

"Yes. I told her you got hurt a little."

"Was she scared and upset?"

Thomas nodded, his face still unnaturally grave. "Yes. I tried to tell her gently, but she's so intuitive. I must not have done a good job. She was crying on the phone." He glanced away, as if the memory pained him.

She closed her eyes, still feeling overly emotional—probably intensified by the head injury. She hated the thought of Mia being so upset and so far away from her.

Then she sensed a warm pressure on her upper arm that was strangely soothing. Thomas had reached over and put his hand on her arm. "She seemed all right when we hung up. I thought... I thought I should prepare her as much as I could. I didn't know when you'd wake up."

Abigail nodded, even though the small move hurt her brutally pounding head. "Thank you." Her eyes burned with emotion she still tried to hold back. "They'll come here?"

Thomas stroked her shoulder gently. "Yes. I talked to the nurse, and Mia can see you. I can call as soon as you're up to it, and my parents will bring her over."

Abigail tossed her aching head restlessly and hoped Mia was okay.

With one last squeeze of her arm, Thomas cleared his throat and stood up. He reached for his phone. "I need to let someone know you're awake. The doctor will want to check you out. But if you feel up to it, I don't see why you shouldn't talk to Mia first."

Thomas helped her position the phone next to her ear, and Abigail held it in place with her good arm, which unfortunately was her left one. She tried to smile her thanks at Thomas before he left the room.

On the second ring, a childish voice said, "Hello. This is Mia."

"Hi, sweetie. It's Mommy."

"Mommy!" Mia's voice broke in obvious joy. "Are you all right? Daddy said you got hurt. He acted brave, but he was really scared. I knew. We're coming to see you whenever he says."

"I know, sweetie. I'll be so happy to see you. I hurt myself a little, but I'm all right."

"Does it hurt real bad?"

"Not too bad. I have a headache, and I hurt my arm. But I want to see you just as soon as possible."

"Okay. I'll tell Grandma now, and she'll drive me right over."

~

The doctor told Abigail she would need a lot of rest over the next few weeks, but she sure didn't get any in the hospital. For the next hour, she was constantly interrupted. First by a nurse checking her vitals. Then by a doctor who performed an examination on her focus and motor functions and then pronounced her as having no signs of serious damage. And then by another nurse, checking her vitals again.

All Abigail wanted to do was hug her baby and then sleep. And instead she kept being nagged and poked and told to look at the light every five minutes.

And to make it worse, Thomas wasn't even with her at the moment to bully away the worst of the intrusions and make sure she was comfortable.

He had gone down to meet Mia and his parents, and she'd asked him to take them for a quick lunch so he could prepare Mia a little more for the way her mother would look in the hospital bed.

Abigail really didn't want her sensitive daughter to be traumatized by her bruised and bandaged form.

She'd just managed to close her eyes when she heard a noise from the doorway and smelled a vaguely familiar male scent.

Before she'd shifted her eyes, she realized the scent didn't belong to Thomas.

Jim Foster stood a few feet from the bed, smiling down at her.

She gasped in surprise, but it wasn't an unpleasant sight. Just not her family, whom she'd really wanted to see. She managed a weak smile. "Hi. What are you doing here?"

"I heard you were in a car accident," he explained, "So I stopped by to see how you were doing. Tell me if I'm intruding."

"Oh no," she assured him, waving with her good hand at the chair beside the bed. "I'm glad to see you. How did you know about the accident?"

"I have my sources," Jim said with an ironic half smile.

"I was just waiting for Thomas to return with Mia."

"I'll leave as soon as they arrive. I don't want to get in the way at a time like this. I was just worried. I'd heard you were still unconscious."

"You need to get more updated sources," she teased him. "I woke up about an hour ago."

He reached out and put his warm hand on hers, which was resting on the bed beside her. "I'm glad."

His hand on hers was comforting, pleasant, but her breath hitched a little. "Jim—"

"I know," he said, interrupting with another wry smile. "You're still married. I might want it to be different, but it's not. Besides, you don't really think I'd come on to you in a hospital bed."

Something loosening in her chest, Abigail gave him a wobbly smile. "I don't want things to get weird."

"We'll make sure they don't."

Abigail was so weak and so relieved that her job wasn't in jeopardy by inconvenient feelings that she might have been smiling like an idiot. "So we're good?

He took her hand to seal the deal. "Definitely."

The sound of someone clearing his throat interrupted their conversation. Both of them turned to see Thomas in the doorway, Mia against his side.

Abigail's expression broke out into a delighted smile at the unexpected sight of her family.

Jim stood up immediately and gave her hand one last squeeze. "I'll leave now. Get better."

Abigail was vaguely conscious of Thomas's level, almost challenging gaze as the other man exited the room. But she was too distracted by Mia—wearing jeans and a pink T-shirt, little glasses slipping down her nose, and two very tightly braided pigtails—to pay much attention when Jim quietly greeted the others and disappeared.

Mia's blue eyes were wide and traveled from Abigail to the departing man.

"Mr. Foster came to say hello," Abigail explained. "But he's leaving now because he knows you're the person I want to see most."

"Oh." Mia nodded gravely, as if this made sense to her. She walked cautiously into the hospital room, gazing around her with what looked like awe. "Daddy said I can't touch anything that plugs into the wall."

"That's very good advice. Did you get something good for lunch?"

"Yes. French fries and chicken strips. Daddy got me a great big root beer too."

"Sounds like I missed out on a good lunch."

"You did." Mia stood next to the bed hesitantly, then looked nervously at the chair Jim had just vacated.

Thomas came over and silently lifted her up into the chair and then pushed it even closer to the bed. "This way you can hold Mommy's hand if you want. It's her other arm that's hurt."

Abigail reached out eagerly when Mia extended her little hand. "Oh, sweetie. I'm so glad you're here. Were you very scared?"

"A little," Mia admitted. "But I was brave like Daddy told me. He said you have bandages on and you have bruises all over you, so you might not look as nice as you normally do. I thought you'd be wrapped up like a mummy!"

Abigail gave a weak chuckle. "So I don't look like a mummy?"

"No. You still look pretty."

"Thank you, sweetie." Abigail looked over toward Thomas and saw him leaning against the wall with one hand in his pocket. She thought he looked more tired than usual and oddly distant.

It worried her.

∼

Late that afternoon, Abigail was alone since Thomas had taken Mia back to his parents' to stay for the night.

She felt sore and drugged and uncomfortable and itchy, and her head was still pounding, and everyone in the world seemed to have abandoned her.

She was just telling herself not to be melodramatic when there was a tap on the door.

As she turned her head and blinked at the doorway, she registered a man standing there.

He was in his early thirties and attractive, and she recognized him immediately. Daniel. The pastor of Thomas's church in Willow Park.

"Hi," she said, her voice sounding strange to her ears. "Come on in."

"I just stopped by to check on you," he said. "But I don't have to stay if you don't feel up to company."

"No, it's fine." She waved him weakly to the chair beside the bed. "I feel pretty bad, but I was also just lying here bored. It's nice of you to drop by. How did you know I was in here?"

"Lydia called me," he explained. "Thomas had told her, of course."

For some reason, Abigail felt a little strange at this news. She didn't like people talking about her, but she could hardly blame Thomas for telling his sister something like this. And news of someone in the hospital always got quickly to the pastor. It was normal. Nothing unusual about it. It didn't speak of any particular intimacy remaining between her and Thomas.

She wasn't part of his church, but Daniel was still just doing his job.

"So did they tell you how long you have to stay?"

"Overnight at least, so they can observe me. I was unconscious for longer than they like. But hopefully I can go home tomorrow. No permanent damage."

"Thank God for that," Daniel murmured. "Would you feel uncomfortable if I prayed for you?"

"Of course not," she said. "Thank you. I can use all the prayer I can get."

So Daniel prayed for her, and Abigail prayed silently, and she appreciated that he didn't try to turn the prayer into a private little sermon aimed at her, the way the pastor she'd grown up with always had.

"Thank you," she said again when he finished and said "Amen."

"You're welcome. Now what can we do for you?"

"What do you mean?"

"I mean, what can we do for you? Me, the church. What do you need from us?"

"Oh," she stammered, feeling awkward and resistant for the first time. "I go to another church."

"I know. But Thomas is part of our church, so we'd like to help too, if you'll let us. What do you need from us?"

"Nothing. I'm really fine." She shifted in the bed, suddenly wishing Daniel would leave. "I don't need anything."

Daniel frowned. "You don't need anything, or you don't want us to help?"

"I don't need help," she said, feeling trapped and too weak to deal with this sort of thing right now. "I don't like for people to help me. I'm really fine."

"Why don't you like people to help you?" The question was conversational, almost casual—as if he was genuinely interested. It wasn't pushy or like an interrogation.

And for some reason, Abigail answered it. "I do okay on my own."

"No one does okay completely on their own. That's not how we were created."

"I know that. I just mean I prefer to be as self-sufficient as possible. I've had… I've had some bad experiences with dependence."

Daniel's forehead creased, as if he were concerned.

Suddenly, Abigail was afraid he'd think she was saying Thomas had been a bully or something, when that wasn't at all what she meant. "I mean my father," she explained. "He was… he was very strict. And very big on authority. He wanted me and my mother to be… to be completely dependent on him and feel ashamed every time we crossed a line. So I got used to never feeling good enough."

Daniel nodded, as if he understood what she was saying.

So she went on, "And then I kind of felt that way in my marriage too. Not that Thomas was ever like my dad or… But when you've spent so long feeling that way, it's hard when someone seems to keep affirming it. Anyway, it's just in the past year that I've felt like I've really worked through a lot of those spiritual struggles." She sighed. "I guess that all sounds kind of crazy."

"No. Not at all." Daniel gave her a sad, little smile. "In fact, my first wife—she died, if you didn't know—my first wife was raised with that kind of background too. She struggled with something similar—about never feeling good enough but always desperately trying."

Abigail felt oddly better, oddly validated—as if her own experiences weren't so strange. "Yeah. That's just what I've had to go through. Anyway, I really do think I'm in a better spiritual place now, but I'm still afraid of falling back into my old patterns. And feeling... feeling dependent seems to drag me back into that old place."

She blushed hotly, suddenly wondering why she'd spilled all that to someone who was practically a stranger. Daniel had probably heard a lot worse, but it just wasn't something Abigail shared.

His dark eyes were sober as he finally said, "I can see how it would be hard for you now to feel dependent if you don't think the help or support comes from love."

Abigail nodded, once again feeling *heard*. "It is. So it's nothing personal or anything. I mean, I really appreciate the offer to help."

"I guess my only question is if you want to stay there after how far you've already come."

"Stay where?"

"Stay where you connect help with shame when that isn't what you were created to be."

Abigail should have been angry or offended since she'd never asked for a sermon or a counseling session. But he wasn't being pushy or offensive. He seemed to be asking an honest question. "I... I don't know. It's easier said than done, you know. To get over... something like that."

"I know it is. But God mends what is broken, and that includes our hearts."

She nodded, believing what he said but not sure what to do with it. She hoped he wasn't going to press the issue since she didn't physically feel up to dealing with it right now.

"I heard Thomas was quite the hero," Daniel added, obviously recognizing the need to change the subject.

"What do you mean?"

"At the accident. The story is going around about how he got you out of the crashed car and had you stabilized before the ambulance came." Daniel was smiling, as if he was pleased with Thomas's crisis management. "Evidently it was a sight to see."

"Oh." Abigail could picture it vividly. Thomas with his cool head and skillful hands and absolute commitment to taking care of her. He would never even tell her about it. He'd never once asked for or expected any thanks for any of the lives he saved every day.

He was so amazing. And it felt like she could see how amazing he really was more now than ever.

Daniel got up, reaching over to pat her arm. "You look tired, so I'm going to take off. I hope you feel better. And please reach out when you feel like you're ready."

Abigail mumbled out a good-bye, and she thought about the conversation for a long time after he left.

∼

"The doctor says you need nothing but rest for the next few weeks," Thomas said in a low, insistent voice. "And you can't use your right arm. And you have to take it easy on your ribs. How exactly are you planning to get by like normal?"

"I'm not planning to get by like normal," Abigail said, trying to think clearly and be reasonable when she was really tempted to huddle under the covers and let Thomas completely take care of her. "But I can get by."

"Can you? You can take care of Mia? Get her to school every day? Take care of the household chores? Do errands? Manage your own care, which I promise will take up far more time than you realize. All with a broken arm, cracked ribs, and the aftermath of a severe concussion?" He was angry. She knew he was angry because his lips had gone white.

"Fuck you, Thomas." She never used that kind of language, but there were no other words to fully embody her feelings at the moment. She was trying desperately not to melt into a puddle of emotion and weakness, and he seemed to be intentionally trying to make it worse.

"Very constructive comment."

Abigail wished she wasn't so dead tired. It was only nine o'clock in the morning. She was supposed to be discharged later that afternoon. They'd only kept her overnight to monitor her symptoms, but she showed no signs of lingering brain injury. Her headache had faded quite a bit, but every other part of her body hurt. And her arm was itching under the cast in a place she couldn't possibly reach.

"Well, maybe you could try to listen to me," she burst out, "instead of charging ahead on your own all the time."

Thomas froze, clearly taken aback by the words. "What?"

Feeling bad about the spontaneous outburst, Abigail glanced away. "Sorry. I didn't mean to sound that way. I know you're trying to help, and I really do appreciate it. But it feels like you're doing your own thing right now and not really hearing what I'm saying."

It had happened over and over again during the years of their marriage—that feeling of her voice not really being heard. She felt a familiar exhaustion rise up at recognizing it yet again—one of those things that wouldn't ever go away.

He sat still for a moment, obviously thinking over what she'd said. Then he leaned forward on the chair next to her hospital bed and reached over to tilt up her chin so he could meet her eyes. "I'm listening now. Tell me."

She took a deep breath, strangely affected by the look in his eyes and the feeling that he really was listening. "I know it's going to be hard, but I don't want Mia to go stay with you while I recover. It will throw off her entire routine. She's upset by all this already."

"I know that," Thomas said, visibly relaxing and lowering his hand. "And that wouldn't be my first suggestion anyway. It would still leave you with the difficulty of managing your own care."

Abigail closed her eyes, the knowledge finally catching up to her that the car accident would have effects stretching out over a long time. "I suppose you want to hire a nurse or something to help me out."

"That would be one option."

"We can do that if we need to, but Mia doesn't do well with strangers. I think it would really stress her out." Frowning, she asked, "What are the other options?"

"You and Mia both could come live with me temporarily." Thomas said the words as if they were natural, as if they weren't of any real significance. "Or I could come live with you."

"What?"

Thomas shrugged off her obvious shock. "It's a logical solution. I'm not a stranger, and Mia wouldn't be uncomfortable with me. My presence could help her through the awkwardness of the transition."

Abigail's belly was suddenly fluttering with nerves, for no good reason. "I'm not sure we should stay with you. I think it would confuse Mia. If we were all living there for a while…"

He nodded. "That makes sense. So what do you think of my staying with you for a couple of weeks?"

She couldn't do anything but gape at him in absolute bewilderment. "I don't understand. You're going to take off work for two weeks to help me do laundry?"

"I wasn't planning to take off work completely. But I can scale back a little—I've got someone who can cover for me now if necessary—and then we can get help from our families. I could be there to help in the mornings and evenings with anything you needed, but I wouldn't be in your hair all day long."

That actually sounded much better than she'd initially thought. And he was right. She would need help. And Mia loved him.

He'd seemed to genuinely hear what her concerns had been and not tried to barrel through them, and that meant more to her than even his offer of help.

She kept hearing what Daniel had said earlier, about her somehow now connecting help with shame in her mind. She didn't want to do that. She didn't want to stay there.

"All right. I think we can make that work. But please try not to boss me around. I know you're used to taking charge, but it's my house. I need to be able to make decisions."

Thomas nodded calmly. "About everything except your health." Before Abigail could argue, he went on, "I know you, remember? I'm not going to let you get in the way of your own recovery because you're too stubborn to see sense."

Abigail glared at him, but because she secretly knew he had a point, she didn't object.

Lifting his eyebrows, Thomas asked, "Any other terms?"

"No bulldozing."

"Understood."

"And there'll be no more drinking wine or fooling around on the couch," Abigail concluded. Despite her wry tone, her cheeks burned at the memory that was still so vivid, even though she'd lost most of the morning that had followed it.

Thomas's mouth twitched up a little, but she thought his cheeks might have flushed a little too. "I wouldn't dream of it."

But then he belied his pious tone by adding, "I'm not sure how well you could balance above me in your present condition anyway."

FIVE

Abigail woke up groggy and confused, conscious of nothing but the pain in her body.

Her ribs hurt every time she took a deep breath, and her head ached with a dull pounding, both on the point of impact and behind her eyes. She had other aches and pains from the cuts and bruises that covered her. Plus she couldn't seem to think clearly.

She tried not to move since moving made everything worse. And gradually her vision cleared and the fuzz dissipated a little from her brain. She remembered leaving the hospital earlier that day, coming home with Mia and Thomas.

Doped up on medication and too exhausted to do anything else, Abigail had gone right to bed and fallen asleep within minutes.

A slight turn of her head showed her it was almost seven. It took her several minutes to figure out that it must be the evening of the same day.

She had to pee, so she started to climb out of the bed. But she almost immediately gasped and froze in place. It just hurt too much to move.

It hurt everywhere—particularly where her ribs were fractured.

The doctor had told her they were only minor fractures and they'd heal on their own in a matter of weeks.

But it hurt like hell. Every time she coughed, sneezed, breathed. Or moved the wrong way.

Abigail was all alone in her bedroom. She couldn't hear any noise from the rest of the house. Mia and Thomas had evidently forgotten about her, abandoned her to her misery. They were probably having a grand time without her.

For a moment, she felt so pitiful she wanted to cry.

She couldn't remember the last time she'd felt so horrible. No, that wasn't true. She did remember.

The last time her body had hurt this much had been when she'd given birth to Mia.

The memory was a little fuzzy now—all the pain and stress of childbirth having blurred over a bit in the joy of finally having her baby to hold. But it had hurt so much—everything had hurt so much—before they'd finally been able to give her the epidural. Thomas had been with her the whole time, but he'd been strangely quiet, strangely stiff. He'd been wearing his work clothes, and pretty soon his shirt was sticking to his skin in a sweaty spot on his belly and in the middle of his shoulder blades. He'd let her hold his hand, however, and he didn't complain or pull it away no matter how brutally she squeezed it.

He hadn't relaxed until she'd been given the epidural and her pain had miraculously faded. Even then, he hadn't said much.

Abigail remembered being so anxious, discreetly scouring every detail of his face, trying to read his expression. Even in the midst of giving birth to Mia, she'd been so scared Thomas wasn't really happy about this disruption to his plans to not have children before they were settled.

So when all of it was finally over, when she held Mia—tiny and wriggling—in her arms, Abigail had burst into tears when Thomas sat next to her bed and smiled.

In that moment, she had experienced hope—as pure and blinding as light—hope that Mia might change the things that felt not quite right between them.

A lump of emotion lodged in Abigail's throat as she forced herself to dispel the memories. The way she felt right now didn't hurt nearly as much as childbirth had.

Of course, there was no joy waiting at the end of it either.

Holding herself very carefully, she tried to pull herself up once again. It was hard with only one working arm and a body that ached with every slight movement. But she pushed through it.

She sat on the edge of her bed for a few minutes, taking breaths as deep as she could bear in an attempt to overcome the dizziness. Eventually, she was able to limp to the bathroom.

Then, feeling utterly pathetic, she made the long, slow trek down the hall. She was wearing a loose T-shirt and a pair of old sweats, and she hadn't looked in the bathroom mirror, too afraid of what she might see.

When she reached the living room, she heard voices from the kitchen, and her heart relaxed a little as she heard Mia say, "Can't we wake Mommy up yet?"

"She needs to rest," Thomas replied, his voice low and mild. "When someone has been hurt like she has, sleep is the best thing for them."

"She's been asleep forever. She's gonna miss the pizza."

"We haven't even put it in the oven. She'll probably wake up before it's done."

Intrigued, Abigail resisted the urge to announce her presence as she made her clumsy way to the entrance of the kitchen. There she saw Thomas's straight back, firm butt, and long legs in his casual trousers and black T-shirt. She also saw Mia from behind. The girl wore a little pair of jeans and a purple top, and she was standing on a chair so she could reach the counter.

Both of them were working on a half-made pizza, and neither yet realized Abigail was there.

"I think that's enough mushrooms, don't you?" Thomas asked, neatly slicing a green pepper.

Mia frowned disapprovingly at her father and kept carefully placing pieces of mushroom on the pizza. "Mommy likes lots of them."

"Okay. What about some peppers?"

"Yes," Mia said, nodding her pigtailed head. "She likes those too." She reached over and started precisely positioning the green peppers in the small spaces left between the scattered mushrooms.

"Should I put the pepperoni on now?" Thomas asked, putting a supportive hand on Mia's back when the girl reached too far across the counter.

"No. I'm making it for Mommy. I'm the one who thought of it to help her feel better."

"Right," Thomas murmured, a slight smile in his voice. "My mistake."

Mia carelessly wiped her hands on her jeans to get rid of the moisture from the peppers. Then she patted Thomas on the shoulder. "That's okay, Daddy. I can do the pepperoni now."

Abigail was torn between snickering and melting into a puddle of sentiment, but she didn't dare do either—since it would reveal her presence and she knew it would hurt too much.

As Mia meticulously laid out the sliced pepperoni on her pizza, Thomas's eyes rested on the girl. Abigail could only see one angle of his face, but his uncharacteristically soft expression shocked her. As did the gentleness of his hand as he reached over to stroke stray wisps of hair back from her face.

"Ouch," Mia said, frowning up at him again. "You pulled my hair."

"I'm sorry. How did I do that?"

"A hair got caught in my glasses," she explained gravely, "And you pulled it."

"I'll try not to do it again."

Mia inclined her head. "Okay."

For no good reason, Abigail's eyes started to burn, and the lump in her throat from earlier returned with even more force.

A few years ago, she would have given anything—anything—to see Thomas be a father this way, to see him act with such obvious affection and show their daughter such focused attention. A scene like this might have transformed Abigail's whole world back then.

Even now, this concrete proof of how much he'd changed was threatening to buckle her knees.

For a moment, she stood in the entrance of the kitchen and practically strangled on emotion. She gripped the edge of the wall and hung on, afraid she might actually fall down.

Then before she'd gotten herself under control, Mia wiped her hands on her jeans again and turned around to hold on to the back of the chair in the process of climbing down. "Mommy!" she exclaimed, when she saw Abigail.

Thomas turned around quickly, obviously taken by surprise.

"Hi, sweetie," Abigail managed to rasp, still too overcome with almost tears to speak naturally. "I finally woke up."

Thomas's forehead pulled together into four little lines as he scanned her face and body.

"We're making pizza for you!" Mia came running over and beamed up at Abigail. "It has mushrooms and peppers and pepperoni just like you like. We have to put it in the oven now, but then it will be ready to eat."

Abigail was still struggling against her flood of emotion, but she tried to smile down at her daughter.

"Are you all right, Mommy?" Mia blinked up at her in concern.

"I'm fine." But Abigail's voice cracked and she suddenly felt dizzy. Her own weakness—both physical and emotional—did nothing to help her desperate attempts to pull herself together.

Thomas did help. He walked over and put a bracing arm around Abigail's waist, skillfully avoiding her painful ribs. "Mia, do you mind running to the bedroom and getting a couple of pillows so we can make Mommy comfortable in the chair?"

"Okay." Obviously pleased to have a duty, Mia scurried out of the kitchen.

"Damn it, Abigail," Thomas muttered, as he walked her into the living room. "Why didn't you ask for help?"

"I'm fine." Abigail shook helplessly now, overwhelmed with everything all at once.

"You are not fine," he insisted in a low, urgent voice. He settled her into a comfortable chair, his hands both strong and gentle. "You're about to fall apart."

Silent sobs ripped up through Abigail's throat, and she contorted her face in an attempt to restrain them.

Thomas's face twisted too. He made room for himself on the edge of the chair and leaned over toward her. "Abigail," he murmured thickly, "Baby, try to pull it together. You're going to scare Mia if she sees you like this."

Sitting in the chair hurt. Crying hurt. Her whole body hurt. "I know." Abigail bent her neck and hid her face against Thomas's shoulder. "I'm trying." She squeezed out a few hot tears against his shirt and breathed in the familiar masculine scent of him.

"Here they are," Mia announced. "I brought…" Her voice trailed off, and with a pang of dismay, Abigail realized why. "Does it hurt that bad?" the girl asked in a broken voice.

"No, sweetie," Abigail said quickly, every maternal instinct in her nature screaming at her to snap out of her little breakdown. "It doesn't hurt that bad. I'm just being silly."

Mia came closer, dragging three pillows and holding the little fan she kept beside her bed under one arm. She peered at Abigail suspiciously. "What's silly?"

Abigail swallowed, feeling more in control now, although still desperately weak. "You remember how I cried at that dog commercial a few weeks ago? That's how I was crying now. It was just so nice to see you making a pizza for me after being away from you in the hospital."

Mia thought for a few moments, the little wheels in her mind obviously spinning as she considered this information. Then her face relaxed. "That's silly, Mommy."

Giving a huff of laughter—although even that was painful—Abigail agreed, "I told you I was silly."

"Thanks for bringing the pillows," Thomas put in, his natural voice moving them away from the precarious moment. "Can you hand them here so I can make Mommy comfortable?"

Mia handed Thomas one pillow at a time. The first he edged between her and the side of the chair to support her broken forearm. The second he used as extra support for her ribs. They didn't really need the third pillow, but since Mia had brought it, he stuck it on the floor beneath Abigail's feet.

"I brought my fan in case you were hot," Mia explained, offering the little red fan like a gift.

Abigail wasn't the least bit hot—in fact, she was grateful for the throw Thomas was tucking around her lap—but she wouldn't have refused the fan for the world. "Thank you. That was very sweet of you."

"Do you think you can get Mommy a cup of water?" Thomas asked, looking over at Mia. "So she can take her pills?"

Mia hurried into the kitchen, and Thomas turned back to scan Abigail's face. He really was very close to her. And for the first time she noticed that he looked strained and little tired, beneath his neutral composure. "You all right?" he asked in an undertone.

It hit her then how incredibly grateful she was that he was here. There was no way she could have managed on her own.

She wasn't sure what she would do without him, even when she was well.

"I'll live," she managed to say. "But if I happen to pass out, you'll carry me back to bed, won't you?"

∼

At nine forty that night, Abigail stood in her bathroom, bracing herself with one hand on the sink counter.

She'd stayed up the whole evening, lounging in the chair in the living room in an attempt to feel a little more human. After dinner, Thomas and Mia had read out loud on the couch while Abigail listened and dozed. Then Mia had gone to bed, and Abigail and Thomas had watched some news.

At nine thirty, when Thomas went to check on Mia and turn off the light, he returned to inform her that the girl was already asleep.

Exhausted and in considerable pain, Abigail decided she would go to bed too.

But first she had to get ready for bed. It shouldn't have been a big deal.

It was.

For one, Abigail still didn't feel very stable on her feet—the pain medication, on top of a blow to the head, left her mind constantly spinning. Plus she only had use of one arm. And bending down in any way caused sharp jolts of pain from her ribs.

But she felt like crap—dirty and disgusting—and she wasn't going to bed until she'd cleaned up a little.

She took out a few washcloths and laid them on the counter next to the sink. Since she hadn't been able to use deodorant that morning, she decided something stronger than water was needed. So she hobbled over to the shower and leaned in to grab one of her bottles of body wash from the ledge.

She lost her balance.

Although she managed to catch herself against the shower wall, the jar to her body hurt so badly that her vision whited out briefly and the line of shampoo, conditioner, intensive hair treatment, and body wash bottles fell with a loud crash into the tub.

Breaking out in a cold sweat and shaking helplessly, Abigail was able to lower herself to the edge of the tub, where she sat and tried not to cry.

A few seconds later, the bathroom door swung open and Thomas burst in.

Disoriented by his sudden appearance, Abigail said the first thing that came into her head. "You didn't knock!"

"What happened?" His face was tense as he looked her over, and there was an expression in his eyes she didn't recognize.

"Nothing."

With his characteristic precision, he took in the strewn bottles in the shower and Abigail's pale, damp face. He squatted down beside her and narrowed his eyes. "Damn it, Abigail. Why the hell won't you ask for help?"

"I really wish you wouldn't barge in here like that."

"I thought you'd fallen." He straightened up and reached down to help her to her feet. "Come on. You should be in bed."

"I need to clean up first." His mild tone after the edge in his voice just moments earlier was just about her undoing. "I stink."

"You don't stink," he assured her absently, bending down to pick up the fallen bottles from the tub. "What did you need in here?" He peered at a bottle of cucumber-and-melon-scented body wash. "Will this do?"

Abigail nodded, once more bracing herself with a hand on the sink. "Thank you," she mumbled when he put the bottle on the counter next to the washcloths. He just stood behind her, so she added, "You can go now."

"You'll either let me help you or you'll go to bed without washing up. Those are your options."

She gasped indignantly at his authoritative tone, but the gasp hurt her ribs. She tried to object to his high-handedness but couldn't find the strength. Instead, she whispered stupidly, "I don't want you to look."

His eyes unexpectedly soft, Thomas moved forward and reached for the bottom edge of her T-shirt. "Baby, I've seen you naked before."

For no good reason, she felt heat flood her face as he gently pulled the T-shirt off over her head and good arm before he carefully maneuvered it over the cast on her right forearm.

She wasn't wearing a bra beneath the shirt, and she felt painfully exposed, even though Thomas's eyes never lingered.

He got one of the washcloths wet and softly rubbed it over her cheek. She gasped at the first contact, but then submitted to his care. Not once could she look him in the eyes as he carefully, efficiently cleaned her face and upper body with the soap and washcloths.

Her cheeks burned with self-consciousness from the intimacy of the act from a man she was no longer intimate with. It would have almost been easier with a stranger—since then it could have been impersonal.

It wasn't impersonal with Thomas, even though none his touches or expressions were sexual in any way.

It was intimate. And it made Abigail feel completely helpless.

When he finished, Thomas helped her put her nightgown on, and then he put toothpaste on her brush and handed it to her.

She brushed her teeth as best she could with her left hand. Then Thomas found her comb and gave her a questioning glance. Since her hair looked like a rat's nest and made her shudder at her reflection, she nodded and let Thomas comb out the tangles.

It felt strangely good to have her hair brushed by someone else. She was trembling now, but she closed her eyes as he stroked the comb through her hair.

Finally, he put the comb on the counter and asked, "Did you want to wash your lower body too?" The first words in almost ten minutes.

She still had her sweats on, although obviously she wasn't planning to sleep in them. "No. That can wait."

"What else do you need?" Thomas's face was unnaturally calm.

"I need to go to the bathroom, but I think I can do that by myself."

After only a brief hesitation, he nodded. "I'll be right outside."

When the door was shut, Abigail went to the bathroom and managed to change her underwear, although it took some effort.

Thomas came back in to help her into bed. And although she hated to admit it, she was really glad of his support as she trudged into her bedroom.

It wasn't just the pain. She felt so incredibly weak.

"Why am I like this?" she asked, after gasping as she tried to crawl into bed.

Thomas arranged the pillows for her. "You have a broken arm," he said, raising his eyebrows, "And two cracked ribs. And you're recovering from a concussion. What did you expect?"

"I didn't expect to be such a wreck. It's like I'm always about to fall over and cry at the same time."

"It's probably partly from the medication, but you need to take it. Cracked ribs hurt like hell." He pulled the covers up over her, positioning her arm so the cast had adequate support.

She made a little whimper she couldn't possibly help.

Thomas reached out his hand as if he would touch her. But he stopped himself and just rested it on the bed. "I know, baby," he murmured. "It won't hurt this bad for long."

The words, his textured voice, were so deliciously soothing that she stretched her hand out to cover his on the covers. She wanted to touch him, to be close to him, and it didn't feel wrong or awkward right now.

He moved his hand to clasp hers, holding it for a minute in silence. And for some reason, that simple touch felt deeper and more real than anything that had happened between them in so long.

She felt another surge of hope that their marriage could be put back together. Silently, she prayed for it—that she could be wise and loving and strong and giving, somehow all at the same time.

Finally, Thomas cleared his throat and reached over to where her prescriptions were set on her nightstand. Carefully reading the labels, he dumped out a pill from one of the bottles. He placed it next to her bedside clock. "If you wake up around two, you can take another one of these. The rest you won't take again until the morning." He straightened up and added, "I'll go get you some water."

He returned shortly and put the water on the nightstand. "Is there anything else you need?"

She shook her head. "Thanks," she said, "Thank you. For helping. I mean it, Thomas. I know I've not been in the best mood today, but it means so much."

"Of course."

Abruptly, Abigail gasped as she realized something. Then winced at the pain the sudden breath had caused. She managed to choke out, "There aren't clean sheets on the spare bed for you to sleep on."

Thomas gave a huff of laughter. "I'll take care of it."

"But—"

"I'll be fine, Abigail. Go to sleep."

She was so exhausted she wasn't going to have a choice but to do as he instructed. But she asked with the last of her energy, "Why... why are you doing this?"

Thomas gazed down at her silently for a long time. Then finally he said, very softly, "I have a lot to make up for. This is just one very small step."

SIX

The next morning, Abigail still felt like crap.

Her mind was a little less fuzzy and she was slightly more mobile, but she had to acknowledge that her recovery wasn't going to be quite as speedy as she'd hoped.

Because she didn't want Mia to think her entire world was disrupted, Abigail let Thomas help her out to the chair in the living room at seven so she could make a pretense of being involved as Mia got ready for school.

Abigail drank coffee and tried not to give in to the urge to complain about her discomfort. Mia brought her clothes out to the living room, and she put on her khaki skirt, long-sleeve white undershirt and Queen Victoria T-shirt while talking to her parents. Then Thomas brushed and braided the girl's long hair and fixed her cereal and juice.

While Mia was eating breakfast and still chatting to Abigail about their neighbor's new poodle, Thomas went to shower and dress.

Abigail recognized that Mia was in a rather clingy mood, so she was relieved when the girl obediently took her dishes into the kitchen when she finished eating. But when Abigail told her to go put on her shoes and get her book bag, Mia stuck out her little chin obstinately.

Abigail knew the morning had gone too smoothly thus far.

"I don't want to," Mia said, crossing her arms in front of her chest.

Keeping her voice calm, Abigail replied, "You have to. You can't go to school without your shoes and book bag."

"I don't want to go to school. I want to stay here with you." Mia's blue eyes were level and defiant, in a gaze that reminded Abigail so much of Thomas.

"I know. But you always like to go to school. I'm just going to be lying around here all day being boring."

Mia came over and clung to the arm of Abigail's chair. "But Mommy, I can help you. I can get you stuff and make sure you feel okay and bring you your pills and everything. Please can I stay with you today?"

Abigail's belly twisted in sympathy. She knew the past couple of days had been hard for the poor thing, and she wanted nothing more than to make her daughter happy. But going to school would be the best thing to ensure that Mia knew her life and routine hadn't completely come unraveled. So she took a breath, summoned the little energy she possessed, and said, "No, Mia. It's nice of you to want to help me, but you have to go to school. Now go get your shoes and book bag."

"No!" Mia was shaking with obvious emotion, and her chin was protruding dangerously. She was usually an agreeable child, but she'd inherited Abigail's stubbornness and Thomas's focused determination. Once she got something into her mind, she was nearly impossible to sway. "I'm gonna stay here with you today."

Abigail swallowed over a lump in her throat. She was just too battered to handle a temper fit this morning, and she knew that's exactly what was about to happen. Terrified she was going to cave to her daughter when she knew she shouldn't, Abigail tried one more time. "Mia, don't be that way. You like school, and then we can hang out together this afternoon."

Mia scowled and was about to make another defiant retort, but just then Thomas entered the living room.

He was dressed for work, having scheduled to go in an hour later than he normally did. She wasn't sure how he'd arranged it, but she appreciated the effort. Without a moment's hesitation, he said, "Into your room, Mia. Get your shoes and book bag. Right now." He didn't raise his voice, but it cracked like a whip, his authority impossible to resist.

Mia crumpled and ran out of the living room to do as her father said.

Abigail crumpled a little bit too. "Now she's upset. This has been so hard for her."

Thomas exhaled and shook his head. "She can't stay with you today, Abigail. You're not in the condition to take care of her."

"I know." Abigail tried to pull herself together. She refused to be a basket case again today. "She needs to go to school. I just wish…"

She trailed off, stopping herself before she said what had been on the tip of her tongue. She couldn't reproach Thomas for speaking to Mia the way he had. He had every right to make sure Mia obeyed. In fact, her first reaction to his exerting his authority had been relief. He was the girl's father. It was his job. He'd simply done what Abigail didn't have the energy to do this morning.

But the authority had also reminded Abigail of her own father, and that brought up all her old baggage

"You just wish what?" Thomas prompted, his expression a little wary.

Before she could answer, she heard the sounds of Mia crying from her bedroom. With a choked sound, Abigail tried to get out of the chair to go comfort her.

"Stay put," Thomas said, his mouth tightening as he turned away. "I'll do it."

Abigail didn't object, mostly because it took too much energy to get up. Shortly, Mia's crying stopped, and a few minutes later the two of them appeared in the living room again.

Mia's eyes were red, but she was wearing her shoes, had her book bag over her shoulder, and was holding Thomas's hand.

"Are you ready to go to school with Daddy now?" Abigail asked.

"Yes." Taking a shuddering breath, Mia slanted her eyes up to Thomas and then continued, "I'm sorry, Mommy."

"That's okay. School will go real quick, and then you and I can be together this afternoon. Maybe we can read or watch a movie."

Mia sniffed and nodded her head. "Okay."

"Give me a kiss good-bye?"

"Okay." Mia ran over and gave Abigail a kiss, and then she took Thomas's hand again.

Abigail mouthed the word, "Thanks," to Thomas with a grateful look.

He shrugged it off and asked, "Do you have everything you need?"

"Yeah. I'll be all right. I'll probably just sleep most of the day."

"Don't try to do anything else." Thomas's gaze was firm and insistent. "No grooming. No housework. Nothing."

Abigail frowned, but at his narrowed eyes, she said, "I'm not going to do anything." With a sigh, she leaned back in the chair. "I don't have the energy anyway."

"Call me if you need anything," Thomas said, with a backward look. "Don't do anything but rest."

"Are you awake?"

Thomas's voice was so soft that had she been asleep there was no way it would have woken her. She shifted on her bed and blinked over at the door. "Yes."

"You have a phone call."

"Oh, I must have left my phone in the living room." Abigail had gone to bed to rest when Thomas got home that evening since she was exhausted from being with Mia all afternoon. She hadn't been sleeping though, just lying in a drowsy haze. She was sure she would have heard the phone ring.

Thomas walked in with her phone. "If you're resting, I'll just tell him to try back later."

Abigail reached out for the phone, wondering who had called her. "No. I can take it."

Thomas tightened his lips as he handed her the phone and then left the room without a word. He left the door open, but that detail barely registered with Abigail.

"Hello?"

"Hi, Abigail," a familiar male voice said. "How are you feeling?"

"Jim. How nice of you to call."

"Just checking on you."

"I'm doing okay. I feel terrible, but I think that's normal. How are things going there?"

He gave her some updates on work, and then he mentioned a luncheon at Milbourne House next Saturday, but he said she didn't need to attend if she wasn't up to it yet.

"I'm sure I'll be fine by then." Abigail smiled into the receiver, thinking how glad she was that any misunderstanding between them had been resolved. "I'll definitely want to be there. I'll see you on Saturday."

She was still smiling when Thomas returned to the room and reached out for the phone. His eyebrows lifted as he studied her face. "Well, that seemed to have improved your mood," he murmured, his tone almost snide. "Are you sure you'll be up for a date?"

Abigail stiffened. "It's work. You don't really think I'd go on a date while we're still married, do you?" She was hurt more than angry, that he seemed to trust her so little. She'd always been completely honest with him about the separation—and it had never been because she'd been remotely interested in another man.

Surely he'd believed her when she'd explained it to him. Surely he knew she'd never loved, wanted, cared about any man in the world the way she did him.

For a moment, Thomas looked almost vulnerable. But then he said in clipped tones, "Of course not."

He turned around and left the room.

~

Thomas was a little distant for the rest of the evening.

Abigail was worried and disappointed since things seemed to have been going so well. During their marriage, it had happened before. Whenever she thought she was actually getting close to him, thinking they were really hearing and seeing each other, he would sometimes pull away. But she'd thought they both had made much progress.

So she spent a lot of time praying and trying to figure out if there was something she should do. They were still on their break from working on the marriage, but she didn't want things to start to decline again.

She watched an animated movie with Mia, and then Mia went to get ready for bed. Then Abigail actually drifted off, waking up and realizing it was nine thirty, so she hauled herself out of bed to say good night to Mia.

She couldn't walk fast, and she'd gotten out of bed too quickly. A wave of dizziness hit her halfway down the hall, and she had to stop for a minute, supporting herself against the wall with her good arm.

Mia would be in bed now, but the light was still on in the room. She'd heard the murmur of voices as soon as she'd left her bedroom and recognized them as Thomas and Mia reading out loud.

But as Abigail tried to recover from her dizziness, the voices took on a different resonance, and she began to make out distinct words.

Mia asked, "Daddy, are you sad?"

"No, sweetheart. Why would I be sad? I love reading with you."

"I don't mean about that." The girl sounded slightly impatient. "But you seem sad."

"I'm not sad."

"Is Mommy not getting better?"

Abigail's hand clenched as she listened, her heart twisting with emotion at the anxious question.

"Of course, she's getting better. She's better today than she was yesterday. And she'll keep getting better every day."

"But she sleeps all the time."

"Sleeping is what makes her feel better. It's good that she sleeps."

"Oh. Okay. Then why are you sad?"

"Mia, I told you I'm not sad."

"But you are. Are you sad 'cause I was bad this morning?"

Abigail heard a muffled sound and then the rustling of the bed. She wished she could see into the bedroom to see what was happening. She knew it was inexcusable to eavesdrop but she needed to hear the rest of this conversation. She *needed* to.

"Of course, I'm not sad about that," Thomas said, his voice a little thick now. "You said you were sorry. It's all over now."

"You're not going to be sad all the time like you used to be, are you?"

"Mia." Thomas's voice was almost strangled for a moment before he composed it. "Sweetheart, there's nothing for you to worry about."

"But I don't want you to be sad, Daddy. If you're sad, then maybe you'll go away."

Abigail covered her hand with her mouth, her vision blurring as emotion ripped through.

More rustling and more muffled sounds. Then Thomas said raspingly, "I'm not going away, Mia. Ever. I'll be here for you, no matter what. Nothing could make me sad enough to go away from you. Sweetheart, you make me happy."

Abigail swiped away a few tears and started limping toward the voices, compelled by the new sound that was unmistakably Mia crying.

When she reached the room, she saw Thomas sitting on the edge of Mia's bed, leaning against the headboard. They'd obviously been reading together since a book lay open and neglected beside them. But now Mia had her face pressed into Thomas's shirt, and both of his arms were holding her against him tightly.

He didn't see Abigail because his face was bent down against Mia's hair.

And Abigail saw something then in the way he was holding her. Something she hadn't recognized before.

Thomas wasn't just comforting his daughter. He was taking comfort from her. He wasn't just giving support and affection. He was receiving it.

He needed Mia as much as Mia needed him.

Another wave of dizziness slammed into Abigail as she processed this new realization. She'd always known Thomas loved his daughter. But the naked need in him she saw at the moment astonished and overwhelmed her.

She stepped back instinctively, knowing that she'd witnessed a moment that wasn't hers to see. Then she retraced her steps halfway down the hall until she finally pulled herself together.

"I think it's bedtime," she called out, as if she hadn't already made it down the hall. "Are you ready for bed, Mia?"

"Yes," Mia replied, as Abigail approached the room. "Daddy was reading with me."

Thomas had loosened his hold on the girl by the time Abigail entered. His arm was still around her, but he was reaching over to pick up the book they'd discarded. "It's my fault we went past nine thirty," he said, his voice composed and natural. "I lost track of time. Sorry about that."

"That's all right. I'm glad I woke up in time to give my good-night kiss." Abigail went over to the bed, and Mia knelt up on the mattress so Abigail wouldn't have to bend over to kiss her and Baxter.

Abigail wanted to hug the little girl, but she couldn't without pain.

Thomas kissed Mia too and then turned out the bedside light. He walked out of the room in front of Abigail.

He was a mature, intelligent, competent man. Lean, strong, and solid—with a manner that nearly always claimed authority in a room.

But for some reason Abigail wanted to cradle him tonight.

~

Saturday morning, Abigail was determined to take a shower.

She hadn't showered all week. Thomas had gotten her some plastic cast covers to waterproof her cast, but between her broken arm and broken ribs she hadn't been mobile enough to effectively shower on her own. And despite Thomas's continued insistence that he'd be happy to assist her, Abigail had kept refusing.

Thomas helped her clean up every evening, but she hadn't been able to wash her hair in a week since her ribs were too sore to bend over or lean back to wash it in the sink. So by Saturday morning, Abigail's hair looked as bad as it ever had in her life.

She wanted to make it to Milbourne House for the luncheon today though, which meant she had to do something about it. It was one thing for Thomas and Mia to see her looking so hideous. The general public was something entirely different.

Her ribs were starting to feel a little better, and she'd cut back on the pain medication that made her so groggy, so Abigail thought she might be able to maneuver in the shower all right. While Mia was eating cereal and watching cartoons,

Abigail and Thomas had an extended argument about her getting in the shower by herself.

On this, she wouldn't back down. And they finally agreed that she'd try it by herself, while Thomas waited outside the bathroom in case she discovered she needed his assistance.

Thomas hadn't yet showered this morning himself, and he wore a white T-shirt and the trousers he'd had on the previous day. Looking heartily displeased with her, he helped her put on the cast cover—which was basically an enormous condom that slipped over her arm and tightened to keep the water out.

Then he said, "I'll be right outside. Call when you finally admit you need help."

She frowned at his use of the word "when" instead of "if," but she bit back her retort and started to shut the door.

"Leave it partly open," Thomas said, appearing both grumpy and domestic in his bare feet and slightly wrinkled clothes.

Tired of arguing with him, Abigail left the bathroom door cracked a few inches before slipping off her robe.

The withdrawal she'd felt in him on Tuesday hadn't lasted. From Wednesday on, he'd acted normal again—at least, the matter-of-fact consideration and dry good humor that was passing for normal with him lately. It was genuinely an answer to prayer.

Since Abigail was starting to sleep less and was able to function more in her usual role, Mia had settled down into her typical routine as well. Things were going fine for the most part. Except Thomas was living with them. And Abigail hadn't showered in a week.

But that was going to change this morning.

Abigail's first challenge was turning on the water in the shower since that required leaning over. She was already breathless and a little shaky when she carefully stepped over the rim of the tub into the shower. But the first cascade of the warm spray over her head and body felt absolutely wonderful.

She stood still for a long time, just letting the water spill over her and enjoying the feel of it after such a long time.

But when she raised her good arm to run her hand through her hair, she gasped with a jolt of pain. The move stretched her ribs in a way that wasn't entirely comfortable.

Determined to endure the discomfort, Abigail made sure her hair was fully soaked. Then she winced again as she reached down to pick up her shampoo bottle.

It was then she realized another complication. She had one working arm. So she needed to squirt the shampoo out into the hand of her good arm in order to eventually get it up to her head. But it was mechanically impossible to use the same hand to squirt the shampoo and receive it both.

She stared down at the shampoo bottle for a minute, water streaming down her face.

Very carefully, she tried to hold the bottle between her casted arm and her side, applying pressure to the bottle to dispense the shampoo into her good hand.

It should have been a workable idea.

It didn't work.

Shampoo did indeed squirt out of the bottle, but she'd pressed it too hard. The shampoo spurted out in a sudden explosion, which she was barely able to catch with her hand. Then the bottle slipped out of its precarious position and fell with a thud to the shower floor.

Abigail bit back a steam of curses, telling herself that she'd done what she needed to do. She'd gotten some shampoo on her hand. There was a thin stream of it running from her palm to her elbow, so she tried to wipe it onto her wet hair. When she'd rubbed it all off, she worked it into her hair with her fingers.

It wasn't enough. It was hard enough to work up good lather with only one hand, but it was nearly impossible with the amount of shampoo she had at her disposal.

Flushed and flustered, she tried to bend over to pick up the bottle to get some more.

A catch of pain from her ribs made her gasp.

Changing strategies, she tried to use one of her feet to push the bottle slowly up the side of the tub. It slipped, so she tried it again. It slipped once more. The third time she tried the maneuver she almost lost her balance.

Catching herself on the tile wall, Abigail gasped in pain and discouragement. For a moment, she felt trapped and helpless—shaky, incapacitated, naked, and with half a head of pitifully lathered hair.

"Thomas," she called, hating to admit defeat this way.

He entered the bathroom immediately. He'd obviously just been waiting for the inevitable. In thirty seconds, he was in the shower with her, just as naked as she was.

Abigail tried not to look.

Thomas leaned over to pick up the shampoo bottle. He poured some into his hand and placed the bottle back on the ledge. "You appear to be having quite a time of it."

When he reached over to massage the shampoo into her hair, Abigail froze. "If you'll just help me get it in my hand, I'm sure I can—"

"Damn it, Abigail," he gritted out, working the shampoo with strong fingers. "What's the problem? I've seen you naked before. I've seen you naked every evening this week. How is this so much worse?"

The answer should have obvious. In the shower, Thomas was naked too.

She released a shuddering sound and tried to make herself relax, knowing it was foolish pride that was making her feel this way and not anything of value. "I'm sorry. Thank you for helping. It's hard for me to feel so helpless, but I really do appreciate it."

At her words, Thomas seemed to relax as well. His fingers weren't soft or gentle, but they felt delicious against her scalp. And it would be so nice to feel clean again.

After a minute, Thomas rinsed off his hands and murmured, "Step back so we can rinse it out."

She stepped back under the spray and let Thomas rinse the soap out of her hair. Wiping her eyes free of water, she looked over at Thomas. Instinctively, her eyes ran over his toned chest and well-defined abs. And then, moved by an irresistible compulsion, her eyes lowered to his groin. She swallowed hard when she saw he was partly erect and forced her eyes back up to his hands.

"I need conditioner," she said in confusion, as she registered he'd poured out more shampoo.

His mouth quirked up, and he didn't seem remotely self-conscious about his nakedness or his partial erection. "I think you need more shampoo first. Your hair was in pretty bad shape."

"You don't have to be snotty. It's not my fault I'm incapacitated."

Arching his eyebrows, he said coolly, beginning to run the shampoo into her hair, "It is your fault you were so stubborn about getting in the shower with me all week."

Sadly, this was the truth. So she had no way to put up a reasonable defense. And now that she was doing it, the whole thing didn't seem quite so bad.

Certainly, it was a little embarrassing. And yes, it made her feel silly and helpless. And of course she was self-conscious about the fact that Thomas's penis had started to harden.

But he hadn't even seemed to notice, and his hands in her hair felt incredibly good. He massaged her scalp as he lathered her up, and the sensation both stimulated and relaxed her.

She breathed deeply, closing her eyes and letting herself enjoy the incongruous indulgence. After they'd rinsed out the second round of shampoo, he reached for the conditioner and gave her the same treatment with it.

The conditioner was supposed to set in her hair for five minutes, although Abigail hadn't intended to wait that long. But Thomas kept up the massage, rubbing his fingertips against her scalp in firm, rhythmic strokes, for what must have been the requisite five minutes.

Abigail couldn't bring herself to make him hurry up. It just felt too good. She breathed in and out with deep, hoarse sighs, barely able to restrain herself from moaning. Tingles of pleasure ran down from her nerve endings and seemed to pulse through the rest of her body.

When Thomas finally said, in a thick mutter, that she could rinse off, Abigail was afraid she'd enjoyed it too much. As she stepped under the spray, she was painfully conscious that her nipples had tightened and a restless pressure had developed between her legs.

It hadn't even been erotic. His touch and words hadn't been sexual at all. What the hell was wrong with her?

To keep her responses from escalating, she asked if he'd pour some of the body wash out in her good hand so she could clean the rest of herself up. She turned away from Thomas as she quickly ran the soap over her shoulders, chest, belly and thighs.

She gasped sharply when she felt Thomas's warm palm on her wet back. And she arched slightly into the stroke of his hand as he soaped up the skin down her spine and along her shoulder blades.

"Thomas!" She gasped when she felt his hand move lower, down to rub her butt and the back of her thighs. Her body responded to the very intimate touch with an ache of arousal she couldn't seem to talk herself out of.

"Since I imagine you won't want to submit to this again anytime soon," Thomas said dryly, with only a hint of gravel in his voice, "I figured we better clean you all the way."

On one level, his words made sense. After the way she was feeling at the moment, there was no way she'd be comfortable getting into a shower with him again. But when he pulled her back under the spray to rinse off the soap, his hands on her wet skin made her want to melt.

She kept her eyes closed as she used her good hand to rinse off her front while he took care of the back. She was afraid to look at him, afraid to see his naked body.

But she knew his appearance by heart. Knew every inch of his body. He wasn't built like a body-builder. The lines of his form and his muscle development were clean and efficient, filled out from his skinniness as a boy but still lean. And she'd always loved the gentle rippling of his arms and shoulders, the firm flatness of his belly, the tight curve of his ass.

"Did you want to shave?"

Thomas's voice broke through her shaky reverie. Her eyes flew open and focused on his face. There was too much water in her eyes and his to really read his expression. "No." There was no way she was going to let him shave her legs in her condition. "Not my legs. But..."

Thomas's eyes strayed down to her groin.

"No!" she choked, instinctively trying to cover the feature in question with her one good arm. "I was just thinking... my underarms... it's getting kind of yuck."

His mouth turned up in a half smile. "Ah. My mistake."

His voice was teasing, and for some reason that seemed to ease a lot of the tension Abigail had been experiencing. She gave a huff of amusement and held out her palm to him. "Soap, please."

She lathered up the underarm of her right side, and when Thomas handed her the razor, she was able to shave the area without any problem. But then she lifted her left arm—her good arm—and realized her problem.

She was absolutely incapable of shaving under her left arm.

Thomas just stood there and cocked an obnoxious eyebrow at her.

"Vindictive bastard," Abigail said without any heat. She could still feel an arousal pulsing between her thighs, but the distractions had helped push it into the back of her consciousness.

"Did you need something?"

"Will you please help me?" she gritted out.

"Of course. Why didn't you ask me before?"

He quickly and carefully shaved her underarm, and Abigail let out a sigh of relief when it was over. "You could at least pretend not to enjoy my humiliation," she muttered, half in jest.

Thomas grew still. "Why would you be humiliated?"

Abigail didn't really have an answer to that. Or she did when she remembered her conversation with Daniel. She was still connecting help with shame in her mind, and it was intensified when it involved Thomas since she'd felt so not good enough with him for so many years.

Instead of answering, Abigail just said, "Thanks for your help. I'm ready to get out now."

She had been vigilantly avoiding looking anywhere but at his face after her first involuntary glance down at his groin. But as Thomas carefully helped her step out of the shower, her eyes accidentally slipped down.

She stiffened dramatically when she saw he had grown from partially hard to almost fully erect.

Thomas grabbed a towel and quickly dried his face and hands before securing it around his waist. Then he took another towel and wrapped it around her.

"See," she mumbled, trying to pull the towel around her nakedness more closely, "I told you it would be weird."

"It's an involuntary physical reaction. Nothing weird about it."

"But—"

"Why are you acting so shy? Do you really think this is the first time it's happened when I'm around you? My body likes how you look. A lot. It always has."

She couldn't help the flush of pleasure. Her body had always liked how his looked too.

But she said, "You've gotten rather obnoxious today." When he just gave her a smug smile, she sniffed. "Must be the hard-on."

"Almost certainly."

~

Abigail had decided she would join the book club. The only reason she wouldn't have done so was because she felt awkward because they were Thomas's friends. But he didn't seem to mind, and it helped that they were getting along better. So the next Friday, the other women came to her house for their monthly book club since it was easier for her than trying to get out to someone else's house in her condition.

The others had brought the food and drink so she wouldn't have to go through the trouble of preparing it.

So far, the evening was going really well.

"He's definitely got the Duncan frown going on," Alice said, holding an infant in her arms.

Jessica laughed, reaching over to wipe a little spit off her son's face with her fingertips. "I know! Sometimes he looks just like Daniel when he frowns."

Jessica's baby, Nathan, was just two months old, and so he'd come to the book club with her even though the other children—Mia and Ellie and Alice's adopted daughter Cara—were all staying with Gabe.

"I was thinking it was Micah's frown," Alice said. She was pretty and quiet and a little shy, and Abigail didn't know her as well as Jessica and Lydia. She was married to Daniel's brother.

"Micah never frowns," Lydia said, leaning back in her chair with a glass of wine.

"Oh, yes, he does." Alice gave the baby a little hug. "And he looks just like Nathan when he does."

"It must run in the family." That was Sophie Miller, the only woman in the book club that Abigail hadn't met before this evening. "I bet if you trace back the history, there will be records going back for generations about the Duncan frown."

General laughter followed this comment, and Abigail was smiling as she went to get a bottle of wine from the kitchen to refill some glasses, which she was managing to do well with her one good arm.

She was surprised that she felt so comfortable, that she was actually having a good time. They hadn't yet talked about the book, but the socializing was casual and enjoyable.

She'd missed this, she realized. Just hanging out with other women.

Sophie had gotten up with her, following her into the kitchen and then checking on the miniquiches she'd put in the oven earlier. Sophie was tiny and dark-haired and really hard to get a good read on. She evidently managed the bookstore in Willow Park.

The quiches were done, so they were working on moving them from the cookie sheet to a plate when Abigail heard Lydia laughing about what a time Gabe must be having with the three girls of different ages, to which Jessica replied he was sure to do a better job babysitting than Daniel, who would probably forget the girls were in the house and just start reading in his study.

Uncorking another bottle of wine and listening to the affectionate dialogue about the other women's husbands, Abigail suddenly felt heavy. Kind of sad.

Because she still didn't quite have that kind of relationship with her husband—one where you could laugh at the other's foibles while completely trusting in each other's love.

Sophie leaned back against the counter and closed her eyes. "Sometimes it sucks."

"What does?" Abigail straightened up, genuinely confused.

"Hearing women talk about their husbands like that."

"Oh." She suddenly realized that Sophie was feeling something of what she felt, although she had no idea why. She checked Sophie's left hand and saw the engagement and wedding rings there.

Sophie must have noticed her look. "I'm married. You haven't heard, then?"

"Heard what?"

"My husband's name is Mark Davenport."

The name sounded vaguely familiar, but Abigail couldn't begin to pinpoint why. "I don't—"

"He was… is a journalist, working in the Middle East. He was kidnapped by Syrian rebels two years ago."

Abigail gasped, so shocked it felt like a slap. It was so far out of her world and experience. "Oh, no. I remember hearing about him on the news, I think. He's your husband?"

"Yeah. I use my maiden now, and I moved back here to run my grandfather's bookstore. We were in DC before, but I couldn't stay there. It's just too much…" She shook her head. "We were only married six months when he left to go over there."

Feeling almost sick with sympathy, Abigail murmured, "He's alive?"

"He's supposed to be. They keep saying they're working on his release. But these things go on for a really long time."

"Shit. How do you even... I mean, what do you do?"

"What can you do? Wait. Pray. Pray a lot."

Abigail was suddenly hit like a sledgehammer with the realization of how she would feel if something like that happened to Thomas, if he were torn away from her somehow.

Because no matter what else existed between them, they were still connected, together, part of each other's lives. Having him lost to her would be like losing a part of her body.

"I didn't mean to make you feel bad," Sophie added with a smile. "It just seemed like you might have felt... I don't know. And I wanted you to know that I understand."

Without thinking, completely spontaneously, Abigail pulled the other woman into a hug.

"It's got to be hard," Sophie said, when they'd pulled apart. "In your situation."

"Not nearly as hard as yours."

The other woman gave a little shrug. "Yeah. But at least other people are supportive for my situation. I bet it's not nearly that simple for you."

Abigail swallowed over a tightness in her throat. "Some people haven't understood. My family..." She cleared her throat. "But a lot of people have been very kind. At first, I thought everyone was judging me, but I really think that most people don't really know what to do. They're used to people divorcing or people staying together—but this in between is harder to... to respond to. I'd probably be the same way if it was someone else."

"That's a great attitude. I'd probably resent all the raised eyebrows. How are things going?"

"Okay, I think. Better than before." Lately, she'd been feeling closer to Thomas, but it hadn't always felt like such hard work. It would be so nice if the endless work could finally be over, if they could just be healed.

That old exhaustion—the feeling of always struggling with no reward—was still lurking in the back of her mind.

"I'm glad." After a moment's silence, Sophie murmured, as if she were talking to herself. "Sometimes I wonder if I'll even know Mark when he comes back. I'm so afraid it will be like there's a stranger in my bed."

"Sometimes with Thomas now, I think I'm looking at a stranger too."

"A better one?"

"Yeah. But I think it's because I'm a better one too."

SEVEN

Abigail felt like doing a jig.

She didn't, although for the first time in three weeks she felt like she might actually be able to perform one. Instead, she just slid into the passenger's seat of Thomas's car.

She smiled at him and said, "Thanks for going to the doctor with me. You really didn't have to."

He gave a half shrug. "No big deal."

"But it must have been inconvenient. I mean, you had to leave the hospital early."

Abigail had taken the afternoon off from work so she could go to her follow-up with the doctor. She'd started back to work at the beginning of the week, having taken two weeks off on sick leave after the accident. Although she was definitely more functional now, she'd been absolutely exhausted every evening after work. So she was really grateful that Thomas had remained living in their little house. She wasn't sure she'd have been able to care for Mia and the daily chores on top of getting adjusted to working again.

But her follow-up visit had been heartening. The doctor declared her ribs in great shape, and he'd taken away the restrictions on physical activities—except those that would hurt her arm. She still had to wear the cast for a few more weeks, but otherwise she was considered in normal health.

"Not a problem," Thomas said.

"Well," she began, staring at his composed face and wondering what he was thinking, "I hope it wasn't a problem.

I really appreciate your staying with us these three weeks. I don't know how we would have gotten by without you. I know you've had a lot of maneuvering to do at work. You can brush it off all you want, but I know it couldn't have been easy."

Thomas met her eyes with a quiet, level look. "I was happy to do it."

His responses kept making her uncomfortable. "Well, thank you. I mean it. And now that all that's left is my arm, you can go back to your place whenever you want."

She'd offered for him to leave last weekend, after the initial two weeks. He'd refused, saying she would still need extra help.

The past few weeks had seemed almost foreign to Abigail, separated and cut off from her real life. She felt close to Thomas in a way she hadn't felt in ages. She'd grown to depend on him—for assistance, for support, and for companionship. Even if it was partly a result of the unnatural situation, she knew it would be hard for her when he left.

She would miss his companionship, his understated humor, his considerate support. She would miss being able to take care of him too.

She'd also been lusting after him for the past two weeks, but that was an entirely different issue.

"All right," Thomas said simply, responding to her offer for him to move back to his place.

Abigail swallowed, a little surprised by his easy acquiescence. But obviously he couldn't stick around forever. It would be better for all of them once things could get back to normal.

They still had two more months before their break was over and they went back to marriage counseling.

"So how do you feel?" Thomas asked, clearly changing the subject on purpose.

She smiled again. "I feel great. I can actually bend over without it hurting." To demonstrate, she leaned forward in the seat of the car to touch her foot with her good arm. "All that's left is to get this stupid cast off."

Mulling over her good fortune, Abigail was inspired by a delicious idea. "Oh, I know what I'm going to do when we get home. I've been dying to do this for the past three weeks."

"What's that?" Thomas asked with a slight smolder in his eyes.

Abigail swallowed hard, forcing her mind away from another thing she'd been dying to do for three weeks. "I'm going to take a bath!"

~

Abigail did take a bath.

Lydia had picked up Mia from school, so Abigail had to catch up on her daughter's day and everything she'd played with Ellie, and then Abigail went to take a bath before dinner. It would probably make more sense to wait until the evening, but she was too excited about finally being allowed to do so, and she'd been so tired lately she'd been going to bed as soon as Mia turned off her lights.

So Abigail drew hot water into the tub, lit candles, and dumped in some lavender-and-honey-scented bubble bath.

Then she sank into the tub and had a delicious soak.

Tried not to think about how nice it would be to have sex.

Since Thomas had been around so often, she'd been slammed with ridiculous urges, sometimes at highly inappropriate times. She wanted to touch him. Wanted him to touch her. Wanted to jump him in the kitchen or in the car or on her living room couch. It had been easier to control the feelings when he wasn't around all the time. But he had been around lately, and she couldn't forget the fact that she and Thomas were married.

They were still married.

But acting on the desire would be foolish since things were going so well during their six-month break. Thomas would probably turn her down anyway, the way he had one mortifying evening the past year they'd been together, when she'd dressed up all sexy in lace-top stockings and lingerie, trying to lure him out of his study and feeling like an entirely new woman than she'd been when she'd met him. She wanted to enjoy being this more confident person. She'd wanted Thomas to appreciate it.

He hadn't. He'd been surprised—astonished really— and then he'd been wary and distanced. Eventually, he'd told her he was busy right now but they could have sex later that night if she wanted.

She'd been crushed and humiliated and deeply ashamed, as not good enough as she'd ever felt. She'd thrown out the lingerie the next day and had gone back to her modest pajamas and nightgowns since even at that point she'd let Thomas's responses change her back into the old Abigail he'd obviously preferred.

But that evening had been very close to the end.

She burned from the memory of that night again as she soaked in the tub. Then she imagined what might have happened if he'd actually responded to her, if he'd liked her to be sexy and confident, how things might have been different.

Her body seemed to be starved for an orgasm, and she was tempted to just rub herself off in the hot water. She didn't though.

The worst punishment she'd ever gotten as a child was when her mother had caught her trying to masturbate at twelve years old and then told her father. Even now, even with all the ways she'd grown and changed, she just couldn't get over that feeling.

She cleared her mind of all that so she could enjoy the rest of her soak.

After she'd gotten out of the tub, Abigail pulled on a robe and brushed out her hair. She stared at herself in the mirror, thinking she looked better than she had for a long time.

That morning, she'd managed to blow her hair dry one-handed for the first time in three weeks. And at her doctor's appointment she'd learned that she'd actually lost five pounds since the accident.

At first, she'd felt too bad to eat very much, and then she'd just been too distracted.

She rubbed lotion on her face and on a whim added mascara and gloss. She smiled at herself, liking how she looked. Then, following through on the random inspiration, she opened her closet and pulled out one of her favorite dresses.

It was simply cut with three-quarter-length sleeves and a heart-shaped neckline with a fitted shape that flared out in a pretty drape. The soft fabric was a silvery blue that almost perfectly matched her eyes. She hadn't worn the dress in years since it had gotten a little snug. But now, as she carefully pulled it on over her cast and it settled over her curves, she felt a silly thrill as she saw that it fit her again.

She twirled in the mirror, feeling like she'd been starting to feel the past year she'd been with Thomas when she'd realized that she could have a sincere faith and devotion to God and still enjoy things like pretty clothes and nice haircuts. It had been a real revelation to her, as ridiculous as it might sound to someone who hadn't been raised the way she'd been.

There was a tap on the door to her bedroom and then a little voice called, "Mommy?"

"Yes, Mia, you can come in."

Mia edged open the door and peered in. "Did you have a good bath?"

"Yes. It was very good. Thank you."

"Ooh!" Mia said, stepping into the room and getting a better look at Abigail. "You look beautiful!"

"Thank you," Abigail replied, flushing a little at being caught in her silliness, even by her own daughter. "I just felt like putting it on."

"It's like a princess. That's the dress you had on in my picture—the one of me when I was little with you and Daddy."

"That's right. I'd forgotten I was wearing this then." Abigail felt a little poignant pull in her heart at the memory of that evening they'd all dressed up to go to a play, when she'd still held out hope for their marriage.

When she looked back over to the door, Mia had disappeared.

Abigail frowned in confusion, wondering where Mia had run off to and why she'd left so abruptly. She was about to go and find her when the girl came running back into the room.

Today Mia had been wearing a casual red knit dress with "Bookworm" written across the front, but as she reentered the room, she was already pulling her dress off over her head.

She was dragging another dress behind her.

"I can wear my pretty dress too!" Mia exclaimed through the fabric as she tried to pull her red dress off without taking her glasses with it.

Abigail was torn between laughter and a surge of affection at Mia's desire to dress up with her.

When Mia dropped the red dress on the floor, she held up the fancy ruffled dress she'd gone to get from her closet. "The one that Daddy bought me. See?"

"I see. Yes, why don't you put it on and show me how pretty it is?"

Earlier that week, they'd gone for a walk to a café on Willow Park's quaint downtown street. In the window of one of the crafty shops that appealed to tourists, Mia had seen this gorgeous, intricately sewn, very expensive lavender dress.

So Thomas had bought it for her.

Abigail wasn't in the habit of buying Mia dresses that fancy since there was almost nowhere for her to wear them and she'd grow out of them so soon. But she hadn't objected to the purchase since they'd had such a good evening together and an occasional treat wouldn't be a problem.

Mia pulled the dress over her head, and Abigail helped her one-handed with the buttons. Then Mia beamed up at her. "Am I pretty?"

Strands of hair were slipping out of the long blond braids, and the wire-rimmed glasses were slipping down on

Mia's nose, but Abigail told her the truth. "You are beautiful."

Clapping her hands in one of her rare, giddy moods, Mia twirled around to make the skirt of her dress flare. "Is your dress twirly too?"

Abigail did a spin to show Mia that her skirt was indeed a twirly one.

They did a few more twirls, giggling and admiring their gorgeousness in the big mirror. And Abigail was momentarily so overwhelmed with joyful affection that she pulled Mia into a tight hug. When the hug ended, Mia didn't let go of her good arm. Holding on with both hands, Mia pulled Abigail into another twirl, this one with both of them circling together, hampered only by the cast on Abigail's arm.

They were both breathless with laughter when they finally broke it off. And they both jumped in surprise at a warm drawl from the doorway. "I thought I heard some twirling going on."

"Daddy!" Mia exclaimed, flushed and merry. "Come twirl with us!"

"I don't think I'm much of a twirler," Thomas said. But he entered the room, his eyes resting on Mia's face with obvious tenderness.

"Aren't we pretty?" Mia demanded, holding up the ends of her skirt to show off the delicate ruffles.

"Beautiful." After spending a minute admiring his daughter, Thomas's eyes shifted over to Abigail, who suddenly felt self-conscious in her dress. "Beautiful."

"I was trying on this old dress," Abigail explained sheepishly, "to see if I could fit into it again. And Mia saw me and wanted to wear her pretty dress too."

"It would be a shame to let such splendor go to waste," Thomas said, idly stroking hair back from Mia's face. "I guess I'll have to take my ladies out to dinner tonight to let everyone see the pretty dresses."

Abigail shot Thomas a sharp look at his choice of language, but he appeared completely unaware of any strangeness.

Mia danced with glee over the spontaneous outing until Thomas said, "We had better leave pretty soon if we're going to get you back in time for bedtime. Run get your shoes on, and I'll call to make sure they have room for us."

"Put tights on too," Abigail called as Mia scurried off to get her shoes. "You'll get cold with bare legs."

When Thomas went to make his call, Abigail walked over to open a dresser drawer. She stared for a long time, but she finally picked up a pair of thigh-high stockings with lace tops. It was probably silly to wear them, but they'd always made her feel pretty. Special. Sexy. Like a sign that she'd grown into herself.

Thomas hadn't seemed to care for them much, but they weren't about him. They'd never been about him, even though he was the only other person who would ever see them.

∼

It was almost ten o'clock when they returned to the house.

Mia had been on an excited high the whole time, and Thomas had been charming and funny. Abigail had a remarkably good time—such a good time that she hadn't hurried along the dinner, even though they were out much later than she usually allowed Mia to be.

While Abigail and Thomas had been drinking coffee, Mia had finally crashed. Then she'd fallen sound asleep in the car on the way home.

Abigail unlocked and opened the front door—then held it as Thomas entered too, carrying a sleeping Mia in his arms.

Without speaking, they went to Mia's bedroom. After Thomas laid her gently on her bed, he started unbuckling her patent leather shoes while Abigail carefully pulled off the dress. She was able to get Mia in her nightgown without waking her, and Thomas turned off the light before they left the room.

"My mother called on the way home," Thomas murmured. "I had better call her back to see what she needed."

Abigail nodded absently. She'd had a glass of wine with dinner and a very indulgent chocolate dessert. She was feeling deliciously relaxed and still far too pleased with the world to take off her dress yet. So she wandered into the living room and slipped off her shoes. She paced restlessly in stockinged feet for a minute until she decided to turn on some music.

She kept the volume low, but she found something with a rhythmic, sensuous sound that seemed to match her mood.

Looking out the window at the small-town street at night, she sketched a few steps, feeling the need to dance, to do something.

She enjoyed the music alone for a few minutes until suddenly a strong arm slipped around her waist and turned her around.

Gasping in surprise, her eyes flew up to Thomas's face. He'd pulled her into a dance position, his arm around her waist. Immediately relaxing and falling into step with him, Abigail moved her good hand up to his shoulder and started to sway her hips with his.

Her broken arm was a little awkward at first, but soon it didn't matter. She and Thomas moved together naturally, intuitively. They'd danced occasionally when they'd been together, but never in the living room without shoes.

Abigail loved it. It was a perfect outlet for her restlessness and her vaguely sensual mood. Thomas's eyes were shadowed since she hadn't turned on the overhead light, but his gaze never left her face.

She felt close to him—after three weeks of living together, after his being there for her in such intimate ways, after his generosity and consideration. And so it felt perfectly natural to move to his rhythm, to press her body against his, to synchronize their breathing.

Thomas's hands had been at her waist, but gradually they slipped down farther. It didn't feel sleazy or presumptuous. She loved the feel of his hands on her bottom, gently guiding her rhythm. And the lean, hard line of his chest felt delicious as her breasts rubbed against it. The sound of the music seemed to mingle with the physical sensations to sweep Abigail away in a sensuous wave.

Eventually, everything felt so good that she dropped her head back and closed her eyes, arching slightly against the heat of his body. And it took her a minute to recognize that Thomas's hands had changed positions again. They'd hiked up the fabric of her dress and were caressing the back of her thighs, just where her stockings met skin.

Thomas's hands were also easing her pelvis into his. The hard bulge she felt at the front of his pants seemed natural too, seemed one more tantalizing feature of the entire experience.

And when his head bent down and his mouth started to move across the exposed skin at the side of her neck, she didn't even question it. She wanted it. Wanted to feel him like that.

When his teeth scraped lightly against her skin, she was suddenly conscious of how aroused she was. Deeply aroused, the pressure pulsing to the beat of the music.

She moaned softly, unable to stifle the pleasure of feeling so incredibly good.

Thomas's hips jerked slightly against her, an uncontrolled move that suddenly jarred her out of her haze.

"What are we doing?" She gasped, still unable to pull away from the warm strength of his body.

"What do you think?" Thomas murmured, throaty and erotic. Once again, he gently pushed his pelvis against hers, and Abigail's intimate muscles clenched in response.

Thomas leaned down again to mouth the side of her neck and said against her skin, "I believe this is foreplay."

Abigail felt a flash of terror followed by a swell of the deepest need she could remember.

Having sex with Thomas was exactly what she wanted to do. He was her husband. She felt close to him again. She wanted to feel closer still.

But it also made her heart race in anxiety.

Thomas raised his head to meet her eyes—his gaze hot, hungry, so familiar. "Abigail? Do you want to?"

She shifted against him, loving the feel of his hard body, the evidence of his desire for her against her middle. "I don't know," she admitted breathlessly.

He opened his mouth to say something, but just then his phone rang from the table beside the couch.

At the sound, Abigail jerked in surprise. Then she released a sigh of relief. "You had better get it. It might be your mom again."

Thomas shook his head, his hands still palming her bottom. "It can wait. She was just asking about some plans for Easter dinner."

She pulled away, needing some space to figure out what she wanted to do. "Get it."

He looked like he was going to object, but then he obviously changed his mind. Pressing his lips together in a tight line, he walked over to pick up his phone, moving a little more stiffly than normal.

Abigail fled, hurrying to her bedroom so she could get away from Thomas for a few minutes and figure things out. There she sat on the edge of her bed and breathed deeply, trying to clear her mind, calm her physical excitement, and recover her senses.

Obviously, she wanted to have sex with Thomas. But she didn't know if she was ready yet, and she didn't know what it would mean for the future.

They had to be so careful. They just couldn't move too quickly.

She wasn't sure how long she sat and mulled over possibilities. Maybe just a minute. Maybe a few. Then Thomas tapped on her door and let himself in without waiting for her response.

He walked over to sit beside her on the edge of the bed. He looked at her with quiet, intense eyes but didn't say anything.

He was still aroused. She could see it in the slight flush on his cheeks, the coiled tension in his posture, the bulge at the front of his trousers. She was still aroused too, even her confusion failing to quench the desire.

"Thomas," she said, her voice a little strangled, "I do want to. I'm just... scared."

He turned toward her more fully. Once again, his mouth opened, as if he were about to make his case. Then something flickered over his expression, and he gave his head a slight shake.

Instead of speaking, he took her face in his hands with an urgency that surprised her. He leaned into a hungry kiss.

She responded, couldn't help but respond. His mouth was passionate, searching, strangely needy. And his hands hadn't released her face, holding it like she was precious. And it was the need she sensed in him more than the desire that dissolved the last of her resistance.

She moaned deep in her throat and twined her good arm around his neck. She opened to the stroke of his tongue, the pressure of her arousal pulsing up through her spine to overwhelm her entire being.

Gently, but with an ardor that surprised her, Thomas eased her back onto the bed as they kissed, and she adjusted to pull her legs up so she was stretched out beneath him.

He was careful about resting his weight on her—probably out of consideration to her recently healed ribs—but she loved the feel of his firm, heated body above her as much as she loved the way his mouth ravenously plundered hers.

Her right arm sprawled out to the side, and she felt at a slight disadvantage since she only had one arm with which to hold him against her, stroke his body. But she rubbed her good hand down the line of his spine until she could clutch at the tight muscles of his ass, trying to push his pelvis down harder against hers.

When he finally tore away from the kiss, they were both panting and slightly dazed. They stared at each other for several seconds, and Abigail was astonished by the degree of hot need visible in his eyes.

"Thomas." She gasped, arching her neck as he lowered his face to trail kisses down her throat.

He hummed against her pulse point, the vibrations making her shiver. Then he raised himself enough to take her breasts in his hands, squeezing them lightly before he caressed down to her hips over the thin fabric of her dress. He'd started to push up her skirt when he leaned down into another kiss.

She sucked his tongue into her mouth and adjusted her hand so she could stroke his hair.

He groaned softly into the kiss, a helpless, erotic sound that thrilled her, causing her to grind her hips up against his.

"Baby," Thomas murmured, his voice muffled as he gave her lower lip a little tug with both of his. "You feel so good."

She arched up into him, as affected by his words as she was by his touch. He'd bunched her skirt up around her waist, and one of his hands had dipped under the lace of her pretty white panties.

"Thomas." She still caressed his head, her fingertips brushing along the curve and ridges of his skull through his hair. "I want my dress off. You need to help."

He gave a choked laugh, pulling up again with a smile she hadn't expected. "So now you're finally asking for my help?"

Despite her deepening desire, which compelled her to squirm her hips against the sensations, she couldn't help but giggle too. "Please?"

He was already sweating a little, perspiration glistening at the center of his forehead and on the sides of his jaw. But his hands were controlled and gentle as he eased her shoulders up so he could reach the zipper of her dress.

When he'd unzipped it, she lifted her hips so he could pull it up past her upper body and over her head. He had to pause to edge the sleeve over her cast, but soon he'd dropped the dress over the side of the bed.

He stared down at her body for a minute even though he'd seen it any number of times over the past three weeks. She wore her lace panties and a matching bra with her thigh-high stockings.

"You're so beautiful," he said thickly, leaning down to mouth his way from her throat to the top of her breasts. When he took a nipple in his mouth through her bra, Abigail gasped at a jolt of pleasure and tried to push her chest up toward his face.

He suckled for a while, fondling her other breast with his hand. And soon Abigail was moaning helplessly and trying to wrap her leg around his body to get some friction where she needed it.

"Thomas, you're driving me crazy." Despite her words, she still had her hand on his head and unconsciously pushed it toward her breast.

He moved farther down her body, mouthing a sensitive spot on her side. He kissed along her belly until he'd reached the edge of her panties.

Shameless and eager, she bucked her hips up toward him, her arousal throbbing now and clenching with excitement as his mouth got closer and closer to where she wanted to feel it.

He nuzzled her through her panties, sliding his hands up to cup and squeeze her breasts.

"Thomas." She couldn't keep her pelvis still and tried to grind it against his face. She was so wet she knew he'd feel it even through her panties. "Please!"

His lips moved deliciously against the lace until he'd somehow managed to find her clit. He applied some skillful pressure, the fabric adding another layer of stimulation.

To her astonishment, Abigail felt an orgasm swell up after about thirty seconds, and she thrashed her hips beneath his mouth as waves of pleasure sliced through her. Biting her lip, she managed to stifle the sounds of her release, making only a few broken mews.

She was gasping as a flush of relaxation washed over her when Thomas raised his head and moved higher up her body. His face was strained, and a sheen of perspiration covered his face, but she saw a gleam of something familiar in his eyes.

"Don't say it," she warned him, feeling more pleased than embarrassed at having come so quickly.

"I didn't say a thing." His lips twitched slightly, however, as he gazed down at her sated face and sprawled body.

"It had nothing to do with any particular skill of yours," she added, just to keep up her end of the conversation. "I've had a long dry spell."

Thomas chuckled as he pressed a soft kiss on her mouth. "I see."

"There's no call for smugness here." Despite her tart tone, her hand stroked his back and head, unable to get enough of the feel of him, even through the fabric of his shirt.

"I wouldn't dream of it."

"You sound rather smug to me." After another kiss, she pushed him up gently, feeling another swell of arousal growing between her legs. "You definitely need to take off your clothes now."

He pulled up immediately and started to hurriedly unbutton his shirt. He undressed in record time. If Abigail hadn't been overwhelmed with a new blaze of desire at the sight of his naked body, she would have been amused by the speed of his disrobing.

"Oh!" She gasped as she stared down at his erection. "I'm not on birth control anymore. We need—"

"I've got some," Thomas said gruffly, groaning as he heaved himself off the bed and pulled his trousers on again. He walked to the door and disappeared, evidently heading into the guest room. Then he reappeared with a couple of condom packets.

"Why do you have those?"

He gave a slightly sheepish shrug as he dropped his pants. "Just in case."

She gasped. "You thought—"

"You're my wife," he murmured. "I wanted to be ready for any possibility."

At another time, she might think this through and have some things to ponder about it. But she was too distracted to think deeply at the moment. Instead, she gazed at him hungrily as he fumbled with one of the packets and rolled on a condom before he moved toward her in bed again.

She hooked the fingers of her good hand around the side of her panties, but Thomas stopped her before she could pull them off. "Leave them on."

For some reason, her desire surged forward at his thick words. She spread her legs, still wearing her bra, panties, and stockings. And Thomas positioned himself between her legs and reached to pull the lace aside so he could align himself at her entrance.

He held himself still, just the tip of her erection nudging her wet flesh. And he stared down into her face. "Abigail, baby."

Her lips parted as she met his gaze, mesmerized by the tone of his voice and the look in his eyes.

Then he pitched his hips forward, sinking into her, his length filling and stretching her.

She was tighter than she'd expected—from having gone so long without sex. And she arched up instinctively at the intense feel of the penetration.

"Oh fuck," Thomas grunted, freezing about halfway in.

Abigail whimpered and lifted her bottom in an attempt to complete the thrust.

Thomas took a few raspy breaths and sank the rest of the way into her, propping himself above her on his forearms and closing his eyes.

"Thomas!" She gasped as the pressure of a new orgasm built up at the big, full, tight feeling of his hard flesh inside her.

He grunted, his jaw tense and his body almost shaking with leashed energy.

Since he wouldn't move, Abigail rocked beneath him, riding him from below with an irresistible surge of desire and need.

"Abigail," Thomas choked out, still holding himself perfectly still.

She knew he was trying to hold on to his control, but that only pushed her further out of control. She pumped her hips frantically, whimpering and panting as her body was washed with waves of heat.

Thomas opened his eyes, and they held such barely restrained need that Abigail arched up dramatically, her whole body shaking as another orgasm crested inside her.

Her eyes fell shut as she tried to muffle her cry of release with the fist of her good hand, vaguely conscious that Mia was asleep down the hall.

She'd barely started to come down, her body softening with delicious satisfaction, when Thomas groaned and pulled out of her completely.

Abigail blinked up at him. "What happened?"

Thomas gave her a tight smile. "You came." Taking a visible breath, he reached down and gave the base of his erection a few squeezes.

"I know I came. Why did you—" She broke off as she took in his obvious tension and the slight shaking of his hands. Then she gave a huff of amusement. "Aha! I'm not the only eager one, I guess. After all your smugness about my orgasms, you're just as eager as I am."

"I never said I wasn't eager." He narrowed his eyes at her, although he was obviously not genuinely annoyed. "But I would have been just fine if you had given me a minute."

"I didn't want to wait a minute. I wanted to come."

Thomas's mouth quirked up. "Evidently."

Abigail couldn't hold back a laugh. She reached up with her left arm in invitation. "Come here, Thomas. I think it's time for you to come too."

He returned her smile and then lined himself back up at her entrance. This time, when he slid himself in, he didn't pause or hesitate.

Her two other orgasms had taken the edge off her desire, so Abigail was able to lie still beneath him and adjust to the penetration as he held himself on his forearms and closed his eyes again. They lay together like that for a minute, until Thomas leaned down to kiss her once more.

She responded immediately, loving the feel of his lips against hers, his tongue moving with hers, his flesh sheathed in hers.

Then he finally pulled away, straightening his arms to lift his chest up from hers. He pulled his pelvis back and stroked in.

With her good arm, Abigail clutched at his shoulder and neck, digging her fingers into his skin as the sensations built inside her. She rocked her hips in time with his, falling into a pleasing, natural rhythm.

"So good," Thomas rasped, his features tight and his eyes hot and hungry. "So sweet, baby. So good."

Abigail whimpered in response, her body jiggling as she pumped up to meet each of his thrusts. After a few minutes, another orgasm tightened at her center, and she twisted and arched against the sensations.

"Fuck, baby." Thomas jerked his head to the side and froze inside her for a minute as her channel started to tighten around his erection.

She bucked and writhed, trying to chase the pleasure. "Thomas, Thomas, gonna come." She'd never orgasmed three times so close together, so she was vaguely astonished at the sensations.

Thomas made an uncontrolled sound in his throat, and then his pelvis jerked roughly against her as his body tensed palpably.

Abigail was on the edge of climax as she saw Thomas's face twist with a sudden rush of pleasure. "Abigail!" he choked as his body shuddered with his release.

He kept pumping his hips, moving inside her, even as he came, and she squeezed her hand down to frantically rub her clit.

The massage combined with his clumsy, primal thrusts, and the thrill of watching him lose control all worked together to push her over the edge. She sobbed out her waves of pleasure as her body convulsed and her inner muscles clamped down around Thomas inside her.

Thomas's elbows buckled, but he caught himself before his weight collapsed on top of her. He was soaked with sweat now, but his face was relaxed and his eyes rich with satisfaction. He eased himself out, holding the condom in place, and then rolled over onto his back beside her.

Abigail felt incredibly good—tired but warm and sated and remarkably pleased with herself. She laughed breathlessly as she turned to look at Thomas.

"Don't say it," he said dryly.

She laughed even harder, feeling oddly giddy as afterglow kept reality at bay. "I didn't say a thing."

"You know, I've had just as long a dry spell as you, but I held out long enough," he said, arching his eyebrows at her in an attempt at his smug look.

"Barely."

When he sneered, she felt a ridiculous wave of affection and leaned over to kiss him on the jaw. "It was great. You were great."

"Thanks. I could have been better, but with three orgasms you did pretty well for yourself."

She recognized amusement in his eyes and perhaps a little glint of embarrassment. "True. I'm definitely not complaining. As long as we both recognize that I'm not the only one ready to come at the drop of a hat."

He snorted. "Duly noted."

With a faint look of disgust down at the condom he still held, he murmured, "I've got to take care of this." He rolled off the bed and paced to the bathroom.

Abigail admired the view of his straight back, lean flanks, and bare butt. Although she cringed in slight embarrassment at the red scratches on his skin from where she'd dug her nails in with shameless enthusiasm.

Her body felt wonderful, but little prickles of confusion and anxiety started to force their way into her consciousness.

She'd just had sex with her husband. And it didn't feel angsty or awkward. It had felt perfectly natural, perfectly right, almost more free of self-consciousness than they'd been when they were together before.

But nothing else about their relationship was perfectly natural and right.

Thomas didn't look troubled as he returned from the bathroom and leaned over to grab and pull on his boxers. He looked tired, and he must have just splashed water on his face. But he smiled at her as he caught her staring.

"Can you grab me something to put on?" she asked, feeling too comfortable to move yet. "From the top drawer there?"

He brought her back a knit cotton nightgown, which she pulled over her head. Then she saw his questioning look and understood it.

She swallowed. "You can sleep with me if you want."

"It's up to you."

He was still handsome as he stood next to her bed in just his boxers, his body toned and his features finely sculpted. But he appeared unexpectedly young, vulnerable, and just slightly uncertain.

Abigail's chest clenched. "Sleep with me tonight."

Without a word, he climbed under the covers with her. He made a move as if he would pull her against him but hesitated. She shifted, closing the gap between them, and she managed to settle herself at his side in a way that wasn't awkward for her broken arm.

He was Thomas. He looked like Thomas, smelled like Thomas, sounded like Thomas.

He looked and smelled and sounded like her husband.

But something about him now didn't feel like Thomas—at least not the husband she'd always been married to.

"I'm tired," she whispered, hating the thought of the discussion she knew was waiting for them.

"I know," he murmured, gently stroking her hair. "So am I. We'll talk in the morning."

Abigail released a long breath and let her body relax, enjoying the afterglow of her orgasms and pushing aside her anxieties for the time being.

She liked the way his arm was wrapped around her, holding her almost protectively.

She'd always felt protected with Thomas.

Leaving that protection had been one of the hardest things about leaving him.

～

When she woke up, her arm felt stiff and her cheek was brutally hot. It only took her a minute to figure out why.

Her face was pressed against the bare skin of Thomas's chest, and her left arm was folded awkwardly beneath her.

She smacked her lips, her mouth feeling rather dry. And she managed to lift her head, the skin of her cheek clinging to Thomas's chest as she pulled away.

A glance at Thomas's face revealed him to already be awake. He looked at her quietly, his eyes unreadable in the dim room.

"Hi," she said, her voice cracking.

"Hi."

"I didn't expect this to happen." She adjusted onto her side so she wouldn't have to sit up.

"Didn't you?" His tone held no particular resonance so it was nearly impossible to figure out what he was thinking.

"No. I mean, I hadn't thought…"

"I had."

She gasped audibly, clenching her left hand. "Wh-what?"

His green eyes were still quiet, but they held hers with unwavering intensity. "I've been wanting this for a long time. I've never stopped hoping it would happen. I don't want to wait until our six months are over. I want to try again now."

He said it so directly, so soon after waking up, that he must have been steeling himself to get it said.

"What?" She gasped, sitting up in bed and staring at Thomas, who was stretched out beside her. Thomas—who had just said what he'd said.

"You heard me. I don't want to wait. I want to try again. Right now."

Abigail gulped, forcing back a surge of excitement and emotion and bone-deep fear. "I know you want to save the marriage, but that's not—"

"It's not just about saving the marriage, Abigail. It's about *you*. I want *you*. I love *you*. I've never stopped."

The words fed something deep in her heart, but they caused a familiar panic to well up at the same time.

She couldn't be foolish. She couldn't melt into compliance just because she wanted so much to be loved by him. She'd done that before, and their marriage simply hadn't worked. It wasn't likely to work now any better unless they were both genuinely hearing each other, understanding each other, in a way they hadn't done before. "It's not that easy to just jump back. Not after everything that has happened."

He leaned forward and grabbed her upper arm in his urgency—but the tightness of his fingers was passion rather than force. "I know. Abigail, I know that. I don't want to jump back. I don't want the marriage we had before. I want a better marriage and family. I think we can do it."

She had absolutely no idea what to say, but she was on the verge of tears.

Thomas cleared his throat, obviously horribly uncomfortable now that he was in the position of baring his soul—even though he was the one who had initiated it. But he pressed on. "I know all the mistakes I made during our marriage. You have no idea how often I've rehashed them over the past months. When you left me, I was... devastated. I was angry, and I felt betrayed. You know I didn't want it to happen, and I didn't understand it at all. I didn't understand *you*. I didn't even really try. I was only thinking about myself—what I thought I needed and what I expected from you. It took me a long time to get through that. But I've been working on it—with God, with myself—and I finally realized over Christmas that the only way to get my family back was to change, to be the husband and father you and Mia need. I know how much I hurt you and betrayed any trust you ever had in me. I knew it would take time. That's why I haven't been pushing things lately—so we both had the time we needed. But I hope I've been showing you that I'll do better this time."

It was a long declaration and a naked one. She knew how vulnerable he would feel, even if she hadn't seen the obvious discomfort in his expression. Despite her fear and confusion, she didn't want to hurt him.

So she took a minute to control her initial reaction—which was to scream at him and burst into tears. Then, "I know how you've changed, Thomas. It's... you've been amazing. You *are* amazing. But that doesn't mean—"

"I love you, Abigail," Thomas said hoarsely. "And I think you still love me too."

She was slammed with waves of confusion, guilt, and fear, and she had to get up off the bed to get her bearings. "But that doesn't change everything that's happened between us or the problems we still need to work through."

Thomas stood up too, so he was facing her. And his expression now was set, almost stubborn. "I know what happened between us as well as you do. But we both believe that God can change people and he can heal relationships.

The past can be overcome, and I'm not the only one who needed this time we took to figure things out."

"I know that. That's the point. I made so many mistakes too. I was always insecure and never felt good enough. We were a mess together, and now we need to be so careful. Jumping into this too quickly might end up hurting us both—and hurting Mia."

Thomas reached out for her again, taking hold of her left shoulder. "Abigail, I love y—"

"Please," she said, interrupting too loudly. "Please don't push. I'm not saying no. I promise I'm not. I'm just saying I don't know yet. We can't rush this."

She felt that deep, familiar exhaustion at the idea of plunging headlong into all the old pain of their marriage.

"I know. But we've had a break, and now it feels like something has changed between us. I don't know why we can't deal with it now." His eyes were urgent, searching, absolutely terrifying. "You don't have to decide anything until you're ready. But I'm not going to stop loving you, and I'm not going to go away."

She was shaking with emotion, trying to figure out what was happening, what she wanted to happen, when she glanced at the clock and saw it was after seven thirty. "Oh no," she muttered, feeling another wave of panic, this one less overwhelming. "Mia."

Without another word to Thomas, she hurried out of the bedroom, still wearing her gown and messy hair. Mia was nearly always awake by this time, and they'd been talking far too loudly, even with the door closed.

Abigail's fears were confirmed when she heard a familiar sound from Mia's room. With a gurgle in her throat, Abigail ran the rest of the way down the hall, nearly leveled with guilt at the sound of her daughter crying.

"Mia," she said, hurrying in to find Mia huddled on her bed, her little body shaking as she sobbed. "It's all right. Sweetie, you don't have to cry."

Mia lifted her head. Her hair was a tangled mess, and her glasses were laying on the mattress beside her. She reached her arms up to Abigail. "Mommy."

Abigail had to stifle a sob herself as she gathered the girl into a tight, one-armed hug. "Sweetie, I'm sorry you're so upset. Everything's all right."

"But you and Daddy are having a bad fight," Mia choked. "I heard you."

Rocking her daughter against her, Abigail said, "We were having a serious discussion and disagreeing about some things, but it's nothing for you to worry about."

Mia clung to Abigail desperately and said, her voice muffled by Abigail's nightgown, "I thought you didn't fight with Daddy anymore."

Abigail's chest hurt so much she could barely stand it. And she hated herself for letting the girl overhear the conversation with Thomas, for not having the sense to stop it before it became so intense.

Taking a few deep breaths, Abigail made herself calm down and think of the best way to handle this. "Daddy and I used to fight a lot, didn't we?"

This question must have surprised Mia. Her shuddering diminished slightly, and she raised her head to peer up into Abigail's face. She nodded soberly.

"We get along better now. But occasionally even grown-ups disagree about things. We're not really mad at each other this time though."

Mia sniffed. "Really? Daddy's not going to go away?"

Abigail managed to overcome a flare of anxiety to say gently, "He's going to go back to his own house pretty soon, but he's going to be around just like he was before."

"Oh." Mia's angst seemed to have eased some at her mother's presence and reassurance, and she wiped her eyes on her forearms and reached to put her glasses back on. "I was hoping he might live with us for good."

"Mia," Abigail murmured. "We talked about this. Remember? Daddy was only staying with us until I was better."

"But you're better now, and he hasn't gone home."

Abigail would never forgive herself if she'd upended her daughter's whole world by making the wrong decision about letting Thomas stay with them these last weeks. She cuddled the girl closer and frantically searched for an appropriate response.

"I wanted to make sure Mommy was completely better," Thomas said from the doorway. He looked composed and natural, although Abigail could see a few hints of strain on his face. He'd pulled on his shirt and trousers before leaving her bedroom.

She felt a ridiculous flood of relief at his presence and his words.

As he entered Mia's room, Thomas continued, "And I was having such a good time with you that I wanted to stay as long as I could. But I don't live here with you and Mommy."

When Mia reached out for Thomas, obviously wanting to give him a hug, Abigail scooted over on the bed to make room for him. Mia crawled over Abigail to settle between her parents as Thomas propped himself up on the bed. "I wish you did live here with me and Mommy."

Thomas stroked the messy blond hair as Mia leaned against him with such trust and affection Abigail's throat nearly closed up. "I know you do, sweetheart. But we have a good time anyway, don't we?"

"Yeah." Mia sounded resigned rather than content, but it was better than her being upset. Then she straightened up and blinked at Thomas. "Even though you had a bad fight with Mommy, you're not going away for good, are you?"

Thomas made a soft, choked sound in his throat. And his features twisted briefly. But his voice was warm and certain as he said, "Of course not, Mia. No matter what else happens, I'm always going to be here for you."

Mia burrowed into a hug, and Thomas wrapped both of his arms around her.

Abigail fought a new onslaught of tears, but these were from relief as much as emotion.

Thomas appeared to have reverted to his old self—the solid, quiet, considerate presence he'd been before this morning.

Maybe he would step back, wait until their six-month break was over, and give her time to ease into this slowly and not rock the boat when things were going so well.

As if he'd read her mind, Thomas met her eyes and silently mouthed over Mia's blond head, "I'm not going to let it go."

EIGHT

"But I want to see the baby polar bears," Mia said a couple of weeks later, her face crumpling in disappointment as she stared at the polar bear exhibit. They were at the small zoo in Dalton, the nearest medium-sized city to Willow Park.

"I know," Abigail said in her most soothing voice. "But I guess they're not out today."

"But you said I could see the babies."

"I thought you could. They were supposed to be out. Maybe the little cubs aren't feeling well, so they're staying inside until they're better." Abigail felt a familiar strain in her chest as she sought to comfort her daughter all the while knowing a breakdown was imminent.

Mia stared with intent focus at the large polar bear habitat, complete with pond, waterfall, cave, and boulders. Her eyes crawled over every visible inch, as if she were verifying the cubs weren't hiding from her.

She sniffed a few times as her search came up empty. "Why aren't the babies here?"

Abigail put a hand on her daughter's shoulder, wishing she hadn't made such a big deal about seeing the polar bear cubs. Normally, Mia would have loved the zoo on its own merits. But she'd gotten Mia's hopes up, and now none of the usual animals would be of any interest at all. "I don't know. Daddy went to ask about it. Maybe he'll be able to find out when we can come back to see the baby polar bears."

Mia turned big blue eyes up to Abigail, momentarily distracted from her woes. "Do you think Daddy can make them let us see the babies?"

Fighting a cringe, Abigail smiled. "Daddy just went to ask when we can come back to see them. If the cubs are sick, then we'll have to wait."

She had no doubt that Thomas had gone to bulldoze whomever he could in order to let Mia visit the polar bears. As soon as the girl's mouth had drooped, Thomas had turned to walk off, murmuring something about "finding out what was going on." But Abigail didn't want to get Mia's hopes up. And she also didn't want their daughter to get in the habit of relying on Thomas to bulldoze over any obstacle to get her what she wanted.

"The daddy bear is here," Abigail said in a bright voice, pointing toward a furry rear end evident inside the cave. "There's his bottom. Do you see it?"

For a minute, Mia stood on tiptoe and peered in the direction Abigail had indicated, looking briefly intrigued. Then she slumped. "But not the babies."

Abigail felt terrible. Mia had been excited all week about the trip to the zoo to see the polar bear cubs. Thomas had moved back to his own house two weeks earlier, and this was his weekend with Mia. But Abigail had been invited to join them on their trip to the zoo, and she knew the fact that both of her parents were present had increased Mia's enthusiasm for the expedition.

But then the cubs were inexplicably absent.

Mia leaned against Abigail's hip, just on the edge of tears, and Abigail was greatly relieved to see Thomas approaching through the milling zoo crowds.

"There's Daddy."

Mia perked up. As soon as Thomas was within earshot, she began, "Did you find out, Daddy? Are they sick? Can we see the babies?"

Abigail recognized the slight tension on Thomas's face—the tightening of his eyes and lips—that proved his mission had been unsuccessful. But he smiled down at Mia. "The cubs haven't been feeling well, so they're keeping them safe inside."

Mia frowned. "Why can't we go inside to see them?"

"We're not allowed to." Nothing in Thomas's voice showed him to be as annoyed as Abigail suspected he was. "The zoo workers are being very careful with them, so the cubs don't feel even worse. But I'll call to check on them every day, and then we can come right over and see them."

When Abigail saw signs of defiance on Mia's face, she intervened, "You don't want to make the babies even sicker by coming out, do you, Mia?"

Mia's lip wobbled. "No."

"Let's go see the sea lions. They're always your favorites. You can watch them swim and flop around, and I think we might get there just in time to see them eat their lunch." Abigail pitched her voice as optimistic, silently praying Mia would give up her disappointment.

She really didn't want the whole day to be ruined by a temper fit and then resulting discipline.

Mia hesitated visibly, torn between bemoaning her fate and seeking pleasure in the always-appealing sea lions.

To tip the balance, Abigail said, "Remember all the fish they eat?"

Letting out a huge sigh, Mia relaxed her shoulders and nodded resolutely. "Okay." Then she held out her hand to

Thomas. "You should see them, Daddy. They eat a tremendous amount of fish."

Thomas raised his eyebrows and took her hand as they started off toward the sea lions. "Do they? Sounds like they're rather voracious."

"Yes," Mia affirmed. "Vor-a-cious."

The breakdown averted, they all traipsed through the crowded paths to the sea lion exhibit. To Abigail's relief, it was almost time for the scheduled feeding. But unfortunately this meant that swarms of other people had gathered to see it.

Undeterred, Thomas shouldered his way through the onlookers until he'd gotten Mia a place at the railing in front where she could easily see the proceedings.

Staying back some, Abigail had a private chuckle over the way Thomas had carved out a place for his daughter. He'd always been that way for her too—a kind of understated protectiveness that she'd loved.

Still did.

He stayed with Mia for the next fifteen minutes as the zoo staff came out with buckets of fish and tossed them out to the sea lions that barked, dove, and swam in exuberant circles.

Abigail watched Thomas and Mia more than she watched the animals. They appeared to be having some sort of profound conversation about the sea lions or the feeding, and Mia had hooked her hand around Thomas's elbow.

Abigail had no idea what to do about Thomas.

He had been as good as his word. He hadn't pressured her or made intrusive advances after his admission two weeks ago. But even though he wasn't living with them, he seemed to be around all the time. And he would smile at her or touch her in ways that felt very intimate. Sometimes she would catch him gazing at her in a way that made her experience his feelings for her almost viscerally.

She didn't know what to do. She was drawn to him just as deeply as she'd always been—more deeply, if truth be told. And lately it felt like all their negative history had faded into a vague blur.

But she knew it hadn't really gone away, and she was terrified of getting back together with him and having it all emerge again.

Things had been so messed up before. *She'd* been so messed up. But having him back in her life like this felt like half of her had finally been returned.

She didn't know what she was more afraid of—losing Thomas or loving him again.

So for the moment, she was trying not to brood about it. Thomas wasn't pushing for a decision, so she could pray about it and wait until the answer was clearer.

When the feeding ended, the crowds dispersed, but Mia still clung to the rail, beaming as she peered down at the flopping, swimming, and sunbathing sea lions. Now that there was room, Abigail stepped closer, and Thomas stepped back to join her, leaving Mia in front of them at the railing.

Thomas gave Abigail a smile and a quirk of his eyebrows. "Crisis averted?"

With a huff of laughter, Abigail murmured, "Yeah. So no luck railroading the staff into letting her see the cubs?"

"No. I guess they aren't eating much, so everyone is worried about them."

Abigail winced. "Good thing you didn't tell Mia. I hope they get better." She let her eyes rest on Mia's golden braided head a few feet in front of them. And she kept her voice low as she added, "At least the sea lions distracted her."

Thomas casually put an arm around her, easing her closer to him. It felt perfectly natural, and Abigail relaxed against his warm body until she realized their position. Stiffening, she said, "Thomas, Mia will see."

"I don't see the difficulty."

"Well, she might think… I mean, she might get the idea…"

"She might get the idea that we're still in love?" The corner of Thomas's mouth tilted up, and his eyes were soft as he gazed down at her. He still hadn't removed his arm, and it was warm and strong around her back. "Now where would she get that idea?"

Tempted to laugh at his brazenness, Abigail frowned teasingly instead. "You're being obnoxious."

"Is that what you call it?"

"You said you weren't going to push."

"Am I pushing?"

He wasn't really pushing. But his arm was still around her and his expression felt like a caress. It definitely felt like he was pressing his advantage.

She swallowed hard. "I'm still trying to figure it out. I'm so worried about rushing and making decisions before we're ready"

"I know. I don't want to rush it either, but I really think we're ready to start working things out. "His hand slid up her back until his fingers tangled in her hair. "Abigail, I'm not expecting it all to happen magically, but it doesn't have to be the way it was before. Any time you want to talk about it…"

"Okay." She took a shaky breath, picturing how she would feel if she tried to share her heart with him again and he still didn't seem to hear or understand her. It would be almost worse than it had been before since they'd both grown and changed so much.

"Okay," Thomas said, as if he'd understood her hesitance. "The zoo probably isn't the best place for it anyway. Just let me know when you want to talk." His mildness flickered into an unexpected spark. "I'll be here."

Abigail gave him a teasing, long-suffering look that made his mouth twitch again.

They stood in mostly silence, occasionally replying to Mia's happy comments, which she threw over her shoulder at them.

After a few moment's reflection, Abigail asked in a hushed voice, "Do you mind if I ask something?"

Thomas's eyes cut over to hers quickly, but his expression didn't change. "Of course not."

Abigail swallowed, inexplicably nervous. She wasn't even sure why she was bringing this up since they'd just agreed to save discussions like this for later. But she found herself asking anyway. "Why weren't you like this—with Mia—when we were together before?"

Thomas's face went very still for a moment, and he didn't answer immediately.

Sighing, Abigail's shoulders slumped. "See. I knew it was too soon. You don't have to answer."

"I want to answer. I told you I'd talk about it anytime you wanted to. I just never said it would be easy." His lips twisted a little, and he swallowed visibly. "I'm so angry with myself for how I acted back then."

Abigail was suddenly worried it would sound like she was somehow judging him. "You weren't that bad. I mean, compared to a lot of husbands. I don't want you to think I—"

"I wasn't who I should have been. At all. For either you or Mia. The truth is…" They were still speaking too low for Mia to hear. "The truth is I was terrified."

Her mouth dropped open. She'd tried to understand his motivations over and over again throughout the years, and she'd always concluded with everything circling around a core of discontent inside him—about his career, his family, his life, her as his wife. She'd never expected anything like this. "Of what?"

"Of losing her. Of losing you."

She stared, feeling like the world was suddenly tilted the wrong way. "What are you talking about?"

He gave a half shrug and looked away as he admitted, "I've only ever been good at one thing—at school and then later at my job. I was never any good at anything else growing up. I didn't do much with sports. I couldn't socialize well. I didn't have a girlfriend all through high school. I was terrible at relationships."

"But you're… you're so amazing. Brilliant and successful and handsome and…"

He gave a huff of amusement. "Thanks for that, but I'm really not. I was just always the nerd who did nothing but study. That's how I've always felt. Never quite… enough. When I met you, I couldn't believe that someone so sweet and beautiful would be at all interested in me. And then once we got married and it felt like you didn't really want to have sex with me, it just fed my—"

"Thomas." She gasped, making sure to speak low so Mia wouldn't overhear. The girl was still happily watching the sea lions swim. "You know that's not what it was. That was my own issue. You *know* that."

"Yes, I knew it with my head, but it kept feeling like I was part of the reason—because I just wasn't good with relationships. I've never been good at them. Then finally things started to get better, and Mia was born, and I was feeling more secure about us, and then..."

She closed her eyes, realizing what he'd trailed off from saying. She was almost shaking with the revelation of something she'd just never imagined before. "Then I started to change."

Thomas nodded. He seemed almost embarrassed about the admission, and his eyes were focused on the concrete at their feet. "It felt like you were becoming somebody different—someone who could never want me. It was what I'd unconsciously always expected to happen. So I ended up making it happen. I didn't do it consciously, of course. I convinced myself I was focusing on the one thing God had made me good at, the one thing I could really offer. But looking back, I can see what happened. I pushed you away. I pushed both of you away."

Abigail was almost numb with the torrent of emotion she felt. It was like an entirely different story had been told of her life. "I thought you didn't want me to change—to be more confident or look different or anything."

"Maybe I didn't. I felt safer with the way you'd been before—where you felt more dependent on me, like I had more to offer you." He made a gruff sound and pulled her against him. "I'm so sorry, baby, that I made you feel like I didn't want you to be the woman you really are. And then for making it worse when I was too blind and selfish to really hear what you were trying to tell me. I know why it's hard for you to trust me now, and all I can say is I'll do everything in my power not to make you feel that way again."

She hugged him back, too overwhelmed to be happy or relieved or anything but what she'd just learned. "I was so jealous of Jim Foster," he said, after a minute.

She pulled back abruptly. "What?"

"I was so jealous. I knew he was into you, and I was afraid... It took me a while to realize there was nothing there."

"I was never even a little interested in—"

"I know that now. But part of me was still expecting you to give up on me and find someone who was just... better at relationships. It really helped me understand how you used to feel, when you were jealous of the women I was friends with. So you see you're not the only one with issues that keep cropping up."

She smiled at him, too emotional to process it all. Then Mia called them over, so they went to join her at the rail.

Abigail had had no idea what he was going through back then. Absolutely no idea. He'd never shared it with her, and she'd never known enough, seen enough, to help him open up or try to address the root of the problem. She'd just thought he was being cold and selfish based on not being happy with what he had in his life.

Exactly as he'd believe about her.

Glancing sideways at Thomas, standing handsome and poised beside her now, the sun glinting off his brown hair, she couldn't help but wonder what else she didn't know about him.

∼

The following Saturday was the weekend before Easter, and there was a community Easter egg hunt next to the duck pond in town.

Abigail hadn't taken Mia for the two previous years since she'd felt so much like she didn't belong in the town, in the community—but she decided to take her this year.

She'd invited Thomas too, which she never would have done even six months ago. He was on call all day, but he hadn't been called in yet, so he was waiting for them on the sidewalk when Abigail pulled her car into a parking place and got out with Mia.

He wore khakis and looked handsome and casual, a little less tired and stressed than he normally did.

She suddenly realized how happy she was to see that—that he was a little more rested, a little more relaxed. Like he was happier than he'd been for so long.

It made her feel restless and heavy and oddly excited as she admitted she might be part of the reason for it.

He'd always wanted to be married to her. He'd never wanted them to be apart. She'd thought for so long that it was mostly the marriage itself that he wanted and the kind of wife he had in his mind. But he'd said it was more than that. He'd said it was *her* he wanted, even as she was now.

And it wasn't as hard as it used to be to believe that was true.

"What is it?" he asked her softly, as he slid Mia back to the sidewalk after the hug he'd given her.

She shook her head, a little self-conscious at the direction of her thoughts.

He didn't press her for an answer, and he put his hand on her back as they walked toward the center of the park where the children and parents were gathering for the hunt to begin.

Mia was sober as she walked, her hand tucked in her father's. Abigail hoped she wouldn't be too shy to enjoy it, but it was a pretty big crowd, which always intimidated the little girl.

Someone called out to them, and Abigail looked over to see Alice and Micah, Daniel's brother, waving at them with a pretty toddler in a pink dress at their feet.

She waved back, but Abigail suddenly felt a flush warming her cheeks as she realized something she should have thought of before.

Half the town was here this afternoon. People she knew, people Thomas knew. And they were here together. His hand was still resting possessively on the small of her back.

People would wonder. People would assume. The whole town would believe they were back together and their marriage was finally fixed.

She shifted away slightly so Thomas had to drop his hand.

She was so happy and excited about the way things were going with them, but she didn't want to do it in front of the eyes of the whole town.

"Mommy?"

She focused down on Mia, forcing the other concerns out of her mind. "Yes?"

"Do you think I'll be able to find an Easter egg?"

"I think so. There are lots of them hidden."

"But there are lots of other kids here. And some are bigger than me."

"But some are smaller too. They hide the eggs in different ways so big and little kids can both find them." Abigail glanced up at Thomas, hoping for his affirmation, but he had pulled out his pager, which his hospital still used to contact its staff.

She almost cursed under her breath when she saw him glance down at it. He looked over and met her eyes, making a reluctant face.

"It's fine," she said. "Did you get called in?"

"Yeah. I think so. I need to call in to see." He leaned down to kiss Mia. "I might have to go to the hospital to work, sweetheart. I'm sorry if I have to miss your Easter egg hunt."

Mia's expression twisted slightly, but Abigail reached down to squeeze the girl's shoulder. "Okay, Daddy," Mia said, understanding the silent signal and giving him an attempt at a smile. "That's okay."

"Thank you. Let me call in and see."

Thomas walked away, pulling out his phone to call, and Abigail saw Gabe, Lydia, and Ellie, so she and Mia went over to say hello.

When Abigail glanced back to Thomas, she saw he was lowering his phone. He met her eyes across the distance.

"I'm going to talk to Daddy," she told Mia. "Stay with Aunt Lydia for a minute. Okay?"

"Okay."

Abigail walked over to Thomas. "You have to go in?" she asked, feeling ridiculously disappointed. She'd really been looking forward to the day with him and Mia.

"Yes. I'm sorry. I was hoping to have the day."

"It's fine. It happens. Mia will be all right."

He lifted a hand to stroke her cheek with his knuckle. "And you?"

"I'm fine. You're a surgeon, Thomas. It's part of the job. It's really okay. You better get going."

"Okay." His eyes were soft as he leaned down and kissed her gently on the lips. "I'll call you later."

Abigail's hand had settled on his shoulder, and she was aware of dropping it as he pulled away.

She watched him walk back to where he'd parked and was suddenly conscious of the fact that he'd kissed her in front of everyone.

She hoped no one would ask her any questions. She wouldn't be able to answer them.

∼

The Easter egg hunt went well over all. Mia was very proud of the three eggs she found, and she'd even made friends with a little boy who lived a couple of blocks away.

She'd been disappointed that her father hadn't been able to stay, but it hadn't ruined her day.

Lydia and Gabe invited her and Mia to go out to dinner with them and Ellie afterward, and Abigail had had been happy to accept. She really liked both of them, and Mia enjoyed talking to Ellie, even though the other girl was almost four years older than her.

All in all, it had been a good day, although it would have been better if Thomas had been able to stay.

She and Mia got home at around seven, and they changed clothes and settled down to read a book. They'd only gotten a few pages into it when the phone rang.

Abigail reached for it quickly, hoping it was Thomas.

It was.

"Hey," he said, when she picked up.

Even from the one word, she knew something was wrong. He sounded stretched, pained. "Are you okay? What's wrong?"

"Do you think you..." He cleared his throat. "Is Mia in bed yet?"

"No. It's not even eight. What's wrong, Thomas? Did you want to come over? We're both still up." Her pulse was racing with anxiety since something was obviously wrong with him.

"Yeah." He cleared his throat again. "I do. Just give me a little while. I need to..."

When he trailed off again, Abigail put down the book she'd been holding. "You're scaring me," she said softly, as if the lowered tone might hide the sentiment from Mia, who was seated right next to her. "Tell me what's—"

She broke off when she realized what must have happened. Thomas had been called in for a surgery, and there was only one thing that left him broken and incoherent this way.

"We're coming out to get you," she said, knowing immediately what she needed to do. "Just stay there. We're coming to get you."

"Okay. Thanks."

When she hung up, Mia's eyes were wide and scared. "Is Daddy okay?"

"Yeah. He's okay. He had a really hard day at work, so we're going over to pick him up from the hospital. That sounds like a good plan, doesn't it?"

Mia had already jumped up. "Yes. I just need to get my shoes on."

Abigail was wearing a T-shirt and sweats, and Mia was wearing fuzzy pajamas with bunnies on them which she and Thomas had picked out last week—she'd made him buy a matching set for himself—but Abigail didn't want to take the time to change their clothes. They got their shoes, and Abigail grabbed her purse, and they were in the car in less than five minutes.

When they pulled into the parking lot in front of the hospital, Abigail said in a serious tone, "Now, Daddy might not want to talk. He's had a really hard day. So we'll let him just be quiet, if he wants. We'll just be with him so he knows that we love him. Okay?"

Mia nodded, pushing her glasses up her nose. "Can I give him a hug, if I'm quiet about it?"

"Yes. I think he would like that."

She took her daughter's hand as they walked into the hospital, and they found Thomas in his office, slouched on the small couch, his long legs stretched out in front of him.

"Daddy!" Mia cried when they saw him, running over to where he sat.

He reached down to pick her up, and he pulled her into a tight hug. Abigail was touched and deeply concerned as she walked over. Thomas wasn't letting go of Mia. He was holding her like she might slip through his fingers.

Abigail lowered herself to sit beside him, not saying anything for what felt like a long time, until finally Thomas loosened his arms.

To anyone else, he would just look tired, but Abigail knew he was feeling a lot more than that.

"Were you reading a book when I called?" he asked, obviously trying to sound natural as he stroked Mia's hair.

She nodded mutely, her eyes turning from her father to Abigail.

"It's okay," Abigail said. "You can definitely answer him."

"Yes, we were reading, but we'd just started when we had to come get you."

"Thank you for coming. Why wouldn't you be able to answer me?" Thomas asked, a question on his face.

"Mommy said we should be quiet if you wanted to be quiet. Do you want us to be quiet, Daddy?"

"You don't have to be quiet, sweetheart. I'm really glad that you're here." He pulled Mia into another, looser hug.

Abigail felt like cradling him, he looked so utterly battered. She needed to get him home first though. "Are you done for the day?" she asked him quietly.

He nodded.

"Good. Why don't we drive Daddy back to his house? That way he can get to bed soon since he's really tired."

Thomas looked like he might object, but neither Mia nor Abigail let him. They collected his stuff and got him out the door to his office and out of the building and to their car.

Mia was worried about leaving his car at the hospital all night, but Abigail convinced her it would be fine and they could just drive him back in the morning.

Thomas didn't say much on the ride home, and despite his attempt to act normal when they all traipsed in through the front door, Abigail couldn't bear to leave him alone in the big old house.

"Why don't we stay here tonight?" she suggested. "It's past your bedtime anyway, and that way we can see Daddy in the morning."

"That's a good plan," Mia said. "We don't want to leave Daddy alone if he's had a bad day."

Thomas began, "You can go back if you—"

"We don't want to go back," Abigail insisted. "Unless you're kicking us out."

"Of course, I'm not kicking you out." Thomas was just standing in the hall, rubbing his face with one hand.

With this decided, Abigail helped Mia get settled in her bedroom and get ready for bed. Then she and Thomas said good night to the girl and left her reading.

Thomas didn't say anything when they were in the hall alone together. He gave his head a little shake and headed for the kitchen.

Abigail followed him.

She wanted to demand he tell her what exactly had happened, but she restrained the instinct. Instead, she poured them both a glass of water and watched as Thomas gulped his down.

After a few minutes, Thomas began, "It... it was..."

Abigail waited, feeling breathless, so concerned.

"It was a girl. Mia's age."

"Oh, no," she murmured, moving toward him and pressing herself against him. "Oh, Thomas, no."

"I thought I could... I did everything I could."

"I know you did. Sometimes there's nothing you can do. I know that doesn't make it easier, but it's true."

Thomas's arms wrapped around her, as tightly as he'd been holding Mia earlier. He felt hard and strong and human—and needy somehow.

Like he needed her. Desperately.

And she wanted him to need her that way. She needed for him to need her.

"Let's go to bed," she said at last. "Let's just go to bed."

"I'm not ready yet," he mumbled against her hair.

"But you're dead on your feet, Thomas. Please." She pulled away enough to look at his face, and realized why he was so reluctant. So she said, "I'll stay with you. I'll come to bed with you."

His expression broke in an emotion she couldn't quite identify. "Are you sure?"

"I'm sure. I want to come to bed with you."

NINE

Getting ready for bed wasn't awkward or uncomfortable, as Abigail might have supposed.

The master suite in Thomas's big old house was set up exactly as their bedroom had been when they were together. The pile of books on the nightstand on Thomas's side of the bed was there just as it had always been. Different titles but stacked in a familiar order—paperbacks set on top of hardbound, fiction separated from medical-related reading. And there was the same engraved tray on the dresser where Thomas had always put his watch and wedding ring at night.

After he changed into the flannel pajama pants he'd always worn, Thomas went to check that the house was locked up, Abigail stood in the middle of the bedroom and felt like she'd never left.

As her eyes flickered over the tray on the dresser, she noticed a glimpse of gold. Without thinking, she walked over and stared down at what she'd seen.

Thomas's wedding ring, exactly where he'd always set it.

He still wore it. He'd never stopped wearing it, although she hadn't been wearing hers since until recently it had felt like a lie.

Thomas returned then, looking a little more like his normal self. "I got you a toothbrush," he said, handing her an unopened package. "And I guess you can sleep in something of mine if you want."

"Thanks." She smiled at him almost shyly and took the toothbrush. Then she opened a drawer and found one of his T-shirts to wear to bed. She'd known exactly where to find his shirts.

She went into the bathroom and changed clothes. Then she washed up using Thomas's soap and toothpaste.

When she came back, she didn't know what to say, so she just crawled into her side of the bed. She wished there was something she could really do to help him through this day.

He used the bathroom himself and then turned off the light as he got into bed.

"Abigail," he said, rolling toward her.

For some reason, the one word caused a lump of emotion to catch in her throat. With a little sound, she scooted toward him and exhaled shakily when he took her in his arms.

"Abigail," he murmured again, holding her tightly against him, stroking her back and her hair with one hand. "Baby. Thank you for being here."

She hugged him back as hard as she could in her position, hating the tension and angst she could feel in his body and wishing she could somehow soothe it away.

When they'd been together before, she'd never really believed he'd needed her. Not like this. Not in the ways that really mattered.

~

When Abigail woke up, it was still dark in the room, but it must have been early morning. It felt like she'd been asleep for hours.

She was still snuggled up against Thomas, and his arms were still wrapped around her. She shifted a little, but his arms didn't loosen. She tried to raise her head to look at the clock, but Thomas mumbled something under his breath and gathered her against him even more tightly.

She gave up on the clock. It was Sunday, and it didn't matter what time it was. Sunday school didn't start until ten.

Relaxing against him, she let one of her hands run down his spine, then up again until she could caress his head. It felt natural, completely inevitable. She'd always loved the feel of the ridges of his backbone and the tight skin and little bumps of his skull through his hair. She didn't see any reason not to feel it now.

Thomas's body was as hot as a radiator—he seemed to be pulsing with heat. But he was completely relaxed, except for the tight embrace of his arms and the hardness of a morning erection. As she trailed her fingers down his back again, she discovered his pajama pants were riding low on his hips.

She slid her hand to his side and squeezed the firm flesh at his waist, rubbing herself unconsciously against his hard arousal.

He'd been asleep when she woke up—she was certain of it. But sometime in the midst of her caresses he awoke. She wasn't sure of the exact moment, but she became vaguely aware of a tightening in his body. Then his head tilted, and he buried his face in her hair, nuzzling his way down to the crook of her neck.

Abigail's body had already begun to respond to the feel of him against her. And as he mouthed the sensitive skin of her throat, sucking lightly at her pulse point, she moaned in naked pleasure.

Thomas hummed against her skin and adjusted slightly, gently pushing her from her side to her back. His hands slid under the oversized T-shirt she wore, and he stroked the bare skin of her belly until he'd reached and cupped her breasts. As he fondled her, he kissed his way to her face.

Flooded with warmth and sensual pleasure, Abigail arched up into his hands and eagerly took his head between her palms. She pulled him into an open-mouthed kiss, her tongue tangling with his in an attempt to feel him more deeply.

They both moaned as the kiss became more urgent. She rocked her pelvis up against his, finding and pushing into his erection. She was fully aroused now, flushed and hot and wet. So she exhaled in relief when Thomas tore his mouth away so he could concentrate on pulling her panties down over her hips and legs.

She kicked her underwear away and yanked down Thomas's pajama pants, reaching for his erection as soon as it was freed. They were still under the covers as Thomas pushed her thighs apart and lined himself up at her entrance.

She lifted her hips to meet his first thrust, releasing a silly mew as she felt his hard flesh push in.

Thomas made a thick sound of pleasure and pressed his face against her neck, his hips working in small, unconscious pumps even as he tried to even out his breathing.

Abigail hugged him close, holding the back of his head with both hands. The penetration was tight but deeply pleasurable, and Thomas's instinctive motion sent jolts of sensation rippling out.

After a minute, she started to squirm, and she lowered her hands to clutch his ass, her fingers digging into the tight muscles there. In response to her silent urging, Thomas reared up on straightened arms and began to thrust, staring down at her with deep, intense eyes.

Abigail moved with him, their rhythm fast, hot, and needy. Her legs were bent up high around his hips, and she used the leverage from her feet on the mattress to ride him from below.

They were both panting loudly, and the bed shook with their urgent motion. And it wasn't long before the pressure of an orgasm coalesced inside her.

She gasped, tossing her head on the bed as she writhed beneath him. "Oh—!"

Her exclamation broke off as she came hard, clamping down around Thomas's thrusting.

His face twisted. "Yes, baby." The words were choked as he jerked with a few clumsy pumps. Then the tension broke inside him as well.

She moaned, low and long, as her body was washed in pleasure, and she felt Thomas come in spurts inside her. He released a thick exhale as he collapsed on top of her, his weight hot and substantial.

They clung to each other, gasping and letting their bodies relax. After a minute, she felt a gush of moisture between her legs, but she was barely conscious of it. Thomas had softened some, and his weight wasn't yet uncomfortable. It all seemed perfectly natural. Inevitable. Finding each other upon waking.

She felt safe. And deeply satisfied.

She might have dozed off for a few minutes—the whole experience blurred into a warm, sated haze. But the next thing she was distinctly conscious of was Thomas hardening inside her again. She felt him twitch and grow, filling and stretching her inner walls once more.

Humming with unexpected pleasure, Abigail sighed and stroked her way down to his butt.

"You awake, baby?" Thomas's low voice was right at her ear, and he readjusted one of his arms so he could caress her hair back from her face.

"Mm-hmm." She squeezed the firm flesh of his butt encouragingly, hoping to get him to move again.

He rocked into her gently, taking most of his weight onto his arms as he raised his upper body above her.

"Yeah," she breathed, stretching sensually and tightening her fingers on his ass, using her grip to guide his motion to the rhythm she wanted.

It hadn't been long since her previous orgasm, but she wanted another one. Her body was primed and eager, and her hips were already shamelessly moving.

Thomas kept his rhythm steady, slower than before. His eyes never left her face, and she couldn't seem to look away either. Because of his earlier release, he was more controlled this time. His skin was slightly damp with perspiration, and the muscles of his arms and neck were clenched with a primal sort of tension. But his rhythm didn't falter as they moved together under the covers.

Thomas rocked into her until she came. Then he lifted her thighs so she would wrap her legs around his waist.

Eventually, Abigail was drenched with sweat and gasping desperately, but her hips still pumped up against Thomas's eagerly. The only sounds in the room were the jiggling of the bed, the faint slapping of their bodies together, and the mingled texture of their breathing. But as Thomas accelerated his rhythm, working inside her more urgently, she started to make little sobbing sounds as she built up toward another orgasm.

Thomas was finally reaching the edge of his control, and the obvious strain on his face and in his clenched body pushed Abigail even closer to release. She loved the way he made her feel, but she loved even more when he revealed how much she pleased him, how much he wanted her, needed her.

"Abigail," Thomas rasped, falling out of rhythm as his head jerked to the side. "Baby."

Abigail arched up, crying out as spasms of pleasure sliced through her. Then she clawed at his ass when he froze inside her, his body clenched as tight as a fist.

"Thomas!" She gasped, not quite sure why she was saying his name, just feeling like she wanted to say it.

He let out a thick, rough groan as he jerked his hips helplessly against hers. His face flooded with a rush of intense pleasure. He pulsed inside her as he came, and then he collapsed on top of her like before.

Abigail was exhausted, completely wiped out, and a little sore. But she felt wonderfully sated and like it was perfectly natural for her lie under the covers on a Sunday morning with a hot, relaxed, panting Thomas between her legs.

After a few minutes, however, she shifted beneath him. She wasn't in danger of falling asleep again, and she was starting to recognize the significance of the gush of fluids between her thighs.

Plus her legs were losing circulation.

Thomas rolled over, freeing her of his weight. But he stayed on his side next to her, one of his hands stroking her red face.

"Okay?" he asked, his green eyes watchful, even as they reflected deep satisfaction.

"Yeah." Her voice came out as a croak, so she cleared her throat. "I think I must have been half-asleep just now."

Thomas's eyes narrowed slightly. "You appeared to be awake."

Realizing how he'd read her words, she clarified. "I didn't mean I didn't want to... to do that. I did. Of course I did. But we should have used a condom."

He visibly released a breath. "Honestly, I didn't even think about it."

"Me either. But... " She trailed off.

"But what?"

"I'm healthy, of course. I've never had sex with anyone but you."

"I've never had sex with anyone but you either." His voice and expression were both utterly serious, as if he was waiting for some sort of boom to fall.

They'd both been virgins when they got married—raised in Christian homes, saving themselves for marriage. It had seemed normal to her back then, but it hit her anew in that moment, and she realized how unusual it was, how special it felt to her now.

That his body had always been for her alone.

"What are you afraid of, baby?"

"I'm not on birth control."

Thomas was silent. When she dared to dart a look over at his face, she saw that his expression was mild and thoughtful. "I'm all right with whatever happens."

Abigail hadn't been nervous all night, everything feeling so perfectly natural, but now her heart started to hammer. "We can't have another baby, Thomas."

"Why not?"

"Thomas. We're not... fixed."

"Not yet. But you know how I feel about that."

Abigail couldn't stand the composure on his face any more than she could stand the flicker of tenderness she saw in his eyes. He meant it."

She sighed and rolled over. "Oh, Thomas, I'm sorry I'm still hesitating. I'm just still afraid of moving too fast."

Thomas rolled over too, adjusting them until he was spooning her from behind. "I know you're worried. I understand why. I wasn't assuming that this, just now, meant that everything was fixed." He stroked her belly softly under his T-shirt she still wore. "I think things are getting better though."

"Yeah." She closed her eyes and breathed deeply, letting herself enjoy that reality. She probably wasn't pregnant. Given the time of the month, it was highly unlikely. And so this would be just another good step forward.

They didn't speak any further, but their breathing fell into sync, and he kept gently stroking her belly under the T-shirt.

After a while, a childish voice spoke from the hall. "Mommy? Daddy? Where are you?"

"We're in here, sweetie!" Abigail called out, instinctively responding to the plea in Mia's voice. It was bright morning outside now, and Mia would have woken up disoriented and confused. Unable to find her parents when she needed them. A rush of guilt surged through Abigail at how she had been making love to Thomas, brooding over their relationship, when her daughter needed her. "It's all right! We're in here."

It was only when Mia pushed the bedroom door open and padded in barefoot with wildly tangled hair that Abigail realized she probably should have gotten up before she let their daughter into the room.

Mia stared with wide eyes at her parents in the messy bed together. Thomas was still cradling Abigail against him, and he was naked under the covers.

Abigail had no idea what to say—how to explain an arrangement that must be bewildering to their six-year-old daughter. Evidently, Thomas was at a loss for words as well.

Mia stared in silence for a long moment. Then the expression on her face changed. "Mommy?" she asked, "Daddy? Do you love each other again?"

Thomas recovered from the awkward silence that followed Mia's question more quickly than Abigail did. "Can you do us a big favor, sweetheart?" he asked, his voice pitched to provoke his daughter's interest.

Mia's face changed, immediately alert at the shift in dynamic. "What, Daddy?"

"Can you go to the kitchen and turn on the coffee pot? It's all set up. You just need to press the on button. Mommy and I just woke up, so can you do that for us?"

"Can I pour the coffee myself?"

"Maybe. But go turn it on first. It will take a little while to brew," Abigail replied, finally finding her voice.

Delighted by this new task, the girl left the room to scurry down the hall toward the kitchen. As soon as she was out of sight, Abigail and Thomas leapt into action.

Abigail found Thomas's flannel pants under the covers and flung them over at him. Then she dug farther under the sheet as he pulled his pants on. Thomas rolled out of the bed and strode to the bathroom. She heard water in the sink as he must have washed his hands and face. Abigail kept searching, groaning in frustration as she practically buried herself under the covers in her urgent hunt.

"What are you doing?" Thomas asked, returning to the bedroom.

"I can't find my underwear!"

With a soft chuckle, Thomas joined the search, and they discovered her panties kicked all the way down in a corner at the bottom of the bed.

Abigail slid them on just as Mia returned. "I did it!" she announced, beaming with obvious pride at her accomplishment.

"Thank you." She knew she needed to answer Mia's earlier question. She tried to think of appropriate words, but she was still too uncomfortable in a rumpled bed that smelled like their morning lovemaking. She was also rather sloppy between her thighs from two rounds of sex.

Before she was able to think of something to say, Thomas bridged the gap. "Shall we make some breakfast, Mia?"

"Yeah! I'm starving!"

Thomas put a hand on Mia's back and steered her out of the room. "We'll get started while Mommy goes to the bathroom."

"Okay."

Abigail shot Thomas a grateful look. "I'll be right there," she called out before she headed for the bathroom, where she cleaned herself up and pulled on the jeans she'd been wearing the day before. She kept Thomas's T-shirt on.

When she joined the other two in the kitchen, she found them absorbed in waffle making. When breakfast was prepared, they took the waffles with some juice into the sunroom to eat. It was warm and bright in the room, and conversation was light and casual until Mia finally snuggled up next to Abigail on the settee.

Deciding that she couldn't put the conversation off forever, Abigail began, "You asked me a question earlier."

Mia nodded, pushing her little glasses back up her nose. "Do you love Daddy again?"

They were speaking softly, and Thomas was calmly putting breakfast dishes onto a tray, but Abigail knew he was listening.

She understood why he was leaving the answer to her, and she appreciated his sensitivity.

Abigail cleared her throat. "Your daddy and I will always love each other."

Mia frowned thoughtfully. "But do you love him so you want to be with him always?"

"I don't know, sweetie," Abigail admitted. "We're taking our time before we decide. We're going to spend some time together and see what happens." She felt Thomas's eyes on her, but she didn't meet his gaze.

"Oh," Mia said.

Abigail was terrified she was handling this wrong, but she didn't know what to tell her daughter except for the truth. "How do you feel about that?"

"Okay." Mia's eyes moved back and forth between Thomas and Abigail. "Are you going to go on dates with Daddy now?"

"Maybe."

"Oh. Will he take you to the symphony?"

"Maybe." Abigail smiled fondly, vaguely impressed that their daughter was putting the pieces of the situation together so astutely.

"Will you get dressed up all pretty for Daddy?"

Abigail nodded. "Probably. But they'll just be dates. We don't know if that means we'll be together all the time. We'll have to see how it goes."

"Like me trying karate to see if I like it before I sign up for the all-year class?"

"Yeah," Abigail said, tightening her arm around the girl. "Something like that."

"Okay."

Mia seemed content with this explanation, and Abigail finally dared to meet Thomas's gaze. There was a faint questioning look in his eyes that caused a clench in her chest, but he didn't put the question into words.

~

An hour later, Abigail was towel-drying her hair after taking a shower. She turned to look over her shoulder as Thomas came into the bedroom.

He shut the door quietly behind him.

"Is Mia all right?"

"She's reading," he explained. His eyes never left her face, and suddenly Abigail knew what he was going to ask her. "Did you mean what you said to Mia earlier?"

"Uh, yeah. I did, I guess."

He took a step closer to her. "So you're willing to… to take that step?"

"Yes. I want to. A lot. But I think we still need to take it slow. We can't just jump back to how we were. There's still too much for us to work through. And I think we better start up counseling again."

Thomas nodded. "I know that." His voice was soft and his face unrevealing.

Suddenly nervous that she'd hurt him, that he was disappointed by her hesitance, she reached out to take his arm. "Is that all right, Thomas? I know we both want things to get better, but I—"

"Abigail." Thomas interrupted as her voice cracked. Something changed, flared up in his eyes. "Do you actually think I'm disappointed?"

She studied his face again, and this time she recognized what had ignited in his eyes. Her cheeks warmed and she dropped her eyes, self-conscious and oddly delighted by the expression she'd seen there. "Oh."

He gently took her face in his hands. "Abigail."

She looked back up and saw again the blaze of excitement, passion, something like joy. For a moment, she was overwhelmed with shudders of responding emotion. And she admitted, "I'm excited too. But I'm still nervous about it. I don't want to end up hurting you. And I won't do anything to hurt Mia."

"We'll be careful," he agreed. Then his mouth turned up in a tantalizing smile. "So do you have plans on Tuesday night?"

Abigail's lips parted. "Tuesday?"

"I'm not on call on Tuesday night." Thomas chuckled, a warm, delicious sound that seemed to travel through her whole being. "Why do you look so dumbfounded? I was just asking you out."

～

On Tuesday evening, Thomas took Abigail to a small town about an hour away. Like Willow Park, it was a quaint town that had capitalized on its historic downtown and regional charm. Abigail had asked Thomas not to take her anywhere too close since she didn't want to feed the town gossips. So they left Mia with a babysitter and had driven out for an early dinner at a charming inn and then an outdoor folk-music concert on the town green. They even stopped in at a few of the antique and craft shops.

Abigail had a wonderful time. Thomas was excellent company—charming and clearly in good spirits. But he didn't come on too strongly or overdo the flirting. He occasionally put a hand on her back as they walked, and he draped his arm on the back of her seat at the concert. But he acted basically natural, and that helped Abigail feel less self-conscious than she might have been on her first new date with her husband.

It was getting late when they ended up in a bakery for coffee and dessert. Abigail had had a glass of wine with dinner, but she was purposefully going light on the alcohol so she wouldn't be tempted to get carried away by the evening's atmosphere or Thomas's warm charisma. She'd already decided it would probably be best not to have Thomas sleep over that night. She wanted to keep things as nonconfusing to Mia as possible.

But Abigail was feeling absolutely wonderful—happy, relaxed, and pleased with the world in general—as she ate a decadent chocolate dessert on the patio of the bakery and laughed at Thomas's wry banter.

They'd talked some about Mia on the drive out, but since they'd arrived in town they'd been talking about everything from architecture to politics to the new tour guide they'd hired at Milbourne House.

Thomas was just telling her about a bizarre man he'd met in the elevator of the hospital when a female voice interrupted them. "Dr. Morgan!"

Both Abigail and Thomas turned toward the speaker, an attractive woman with nut-brown hair and a cast on her wrist. She wore jeans and a button-up shirt, and her smile widened as she approached "Dr. Morgan. Were you here for the concert?"

Thomas stood up and held out his hand in greeting. "Bethany, it's good to see you. Yes, we drove out for the concert."

Bethany turned to Abigail with a smile. "I hope you enjoyed it."

Abigail stood up too. "Yes, it was lovely."

"This is Bethany Harris," Thomas said, his eyes on Abigail's face. Something in his expression had changed, but Abigail couldn't pin it down. "She's a nurse at the hospital. Bethany, this is Abigail."

Bethany smiled as they shook hands. "It's nice to meet you."

"I'd forgotten you live here," Thomas said casually, stepping over so he was just at Abigail's side. He put a discreet hand on the small of her back as he continued. "It's a charming town."

"Thanks. We've worked hard to make it so."

Abigail was still wondering about the change in Thomas's expression. He was studying her face out of the corner of his eyes, like he was looking for signs of something.

She had no idea what had distracted him, but she could feel in the vibes from his body that he'd tensed up a little.

There didn't seem to be any reason why. Bethany seemed like a perfectly agreeable woman—friendly and natural.

Since Thomas wasn't putting much effort into the conversation, Abigail picked up the slack. "What happened to your wrist?" she asked, gesturing toward the cast.

Bethany made a face. "Fell down some stairs. Very stupid. Now I'm paying for it. I can't believe how many things are nearly impossible with only one hand."

"Don't I know it," Abigail replied sympathetically. "I was in a car accident a couple of months ago, and I had a cast on my arm for eight weeks. How much longer do you have?"

"The doctor said maybe another month. I guess I'll live." Bethany glanced over to Thomas, who still looked rather odd. "Anyway, I just stopped by to say hi. I hope you enjoy the rest of the evening."

"Thanks," Abigail said, as Thomas managed a farewell as well.

As they sat down at their table again, Abigail frowned and studied Thomas's face. What on earth could have caused him to get so uptight? He was still searching her face almost urgently.

"I'd forgotten she lived here," he said, as if in response to a piece of conversation Abigail had missed.

Abigail blinked. "That's what you said before. No reason for you to remember. There must be millions of nurses at the hospital."

Thomas's eyes narrowed, and something changed on his face. But he said lightly, "That might be a slight exaggeration."

She chuckled. "Maybe. But what got into you? Do you not like her? She seemed really nice."

"She's fine," Thomas said, still focused as if he were trying to peer into Abigail's soul. "She's good at her job. I don't know her very well."

Abigail shrugged. "Anyway, you were telling me about that crazy man on the elevator."

Thomas leaned back in his chair and stared at her for a moment, as if he were silently astounded.

Growing self-conscious and absolutely bewildered, Abigail demanded, "What the heck is the matter with you, Thomas?"

"Nothing," Thomas assured her, his face clearing of its inexplicable distraction. "Sorry. I was just thinking about something else."

Abigail watched him thoughtfully as he finished his story. But she concluded that—whatever the thing had been—it was temporary and not very important. It hadn't really altered the mood between them.

If anything, Thomas's expression now was warmer and fonder than before.

~

It was late when they got back, and Thomas walked with her to the front door of her house.

She felt warm and fluttery, the way she had after their very first date, when he'd brought her flowers, taken her out to dinner back in Durham, and asked very earnestly if he could see her again.

"Did you want to come in?" she asked, glancing over her shoulder to the front window. The lights were flickering, so the babysitter obviously had the television on.

Thomas shook his head, his eyes deep and soft. "If I come in, I'll want to stay."

She felt her heart speed up, realizing that she wanted him to stay too. She would love to take him to bed right now. But they'd agreed to take it slow, and she didn't want to get caught up in the enjoyment of sex and fail to ensure the rest of their relationship was on track. So she said, "Okay. I guess it's pretty late."

"I'll call you tomorrow."

"Thank you for tonight. I really enjoyed it."

She saw his expression shift as he leaned toward her, and she stretched up to meet him halfway as his lips pressed very gently against hers. "I did too," he murmured against her mouth.

She reached her arms up to wrap around his neck, and he pulled her into a tight hug. It felt like his strength and affection was surrounding her, embracing her.

When she pulled away, she couldn't help but say, "Can I ask you something?"

"Of course. Anything."

"Why were you acting so weird this evening, when we ran into Bethany?" The weirdness had totally dissipated, but the question still lingered in her mind.

He cleared his throat and glanced down at the front step before he lifted his eyes to admit, "I was afraid you might get jealous."

She blinked a couple of times. "Jealous? Of Bethany? Wh—" She broke off her question as she realized the answer. She let her breath out in a rush. "Oh. Of course. I would have gotten all jealous and insecure before."

"Maybe I was wrong to worry, but I didn't want anything to get in the way of how things are going between us right now. So I…" Thomas gave a sheepish shrug.

"Yeah. It's funny, but it never even occurred to me to be jealous tonight." She felt a deep swell of hope at the realization of how different things felt now.

Maybe she'd really changed. Maybe she'd actually won a victory over the spiritual battle she'd been fighting for so many years about never feeling good enough. Maybe she could finally stop working, trying, making sure all the baggage from her past didn't make her into someone she wasn't. Maybe this meant their marriage wouldn't have to be a constant, uphill battle.

She felt so much hope and joy that all she could say was, "I think that's a good sign."

"Of course it's a good sign. It means so much that you trust me."

She could tell that he meant it, and it sent a ripple of concern through her heart. "It's not that I ever really thought you would cheat on me, Thomas. I hope you know that. It was just part of how I always felt not good enough, and the idea of other women who seemed to have more to offer than me just confirmed the feeling."

"I understand that now."

"Back then you didn't?"

He shook his head with an expression that was almost tired. "Back then I assumed it was another sign that I wasn't any good at relationships and you were slowly pulling away from me. I hope you understand that I felt just as not good enough as you did. It just took a different form."

"I didn't know that before," she admitted. "It never even occurred to me. But I'm starting to realize it now."

He reached out to pull her into another hug, and they stood together in the embrace for a long time on the front step of her little house.

When they finally pulled apart, Abigail had to force herself to go inside before she grabbed hold of Thomas and dragged him inside with her for the night.

TEN

On Friday, Abigail was cleaning up after a quick dinner—fit between Thomas arriving after work and their all leaving for the Good Friday service at church. She'd wanted it to be a family occasion, so they were all going to Willow Park Church.

She was seriously thinking about starting to go there all the time since it was a better fit for her as a church and Thomas's attendance was no longer an obstacle.

At the moment, she was listening to the conversation in the dining room where Thomas and Mia were playing Thomas's old board game of Operation, which he'd dug out of his attic earlier that week.

They were both utterly serious about each move they made, and Abigail had a few private giggles as she listened.

"Oh, no," Mia said, after several seconds of silence and then a familiar buzzing sound. "I messed up."

"That's okay. It takes a lot of practice to keep your hand really still."

"Did you practice a lot when you were a kid? Did you and Aunt Lydia play?"

"I played a lot, but Aunt Lydia didn't really like it. She always said it was mostly boring with just a few seconds of excitement. She liked to play sports and more active games."

"Oh." Mia clearly thought about this for a while before she continued, "Did you like to play sports and more active games too?"

"Not really. I swam on a swim team, but I didn't really like it. I mostly liked school and books."

"Me too. That's what I like too."

"Well, we're alike in that then. I was on the chess team though. I liked that."

"Do you think I would like chess, Daddy?"

"You might. I can teach you sometime if you want."

Abigail shook her head, already imagining the intense chess tournaments between the two of them in the future.

"One of the girls in my class said that girls who like to read all the time are boring and not popular. Do you think that's true, Daddy?"

Abigail stiffened in instinctive resentment at the girl who had made Mia feel bad about herself. Mia hadn't told her about it, and she wished she'd known it earlier.

"No. I don't think that's true. But I don't think being popular is really that important anyway."

"Why not?"

"Because it doesn't mean you're happy or not. It doesn't mean people really love you. Your Aunt Lydia was always really popular in school, and I was never popular at all. But we're both happy now, and we have people who love us. And God loves us both just as much. I think that's what matters more than being popular."

"Oh." Mia was obviously mulling over this bit of wisdom, the way she always did before she spoke. "I think so too."

Abigail felt her chest relax at the peace in her daughter's voice, and she felt a tug of affection for Thomas with his matter-of-fact sincerity in handling the issue.

It was funny. She always thought about Thomas as he was now—handsome, successfully, brilliant, composed, and seemingly confident. She'd never thought about him as a boy. But he would have been supersmart, reserved, academic, and focused, none of them traits that led to popularity in school. He'd called himself a nerd, and that was how other kids had probably seen him.

She'd never even considered until recently. When they'd talked about their childhoods, he'd told her about his family and about the ways he'd excelled in academics. He'd never told her about not being popular. She'd never imagined he would have any reason to be insecure. About anything.

The game playing continued from the dining room, and she was finishing loading the dishwasher when she heard Mia say, "You're really good at this, Daddy."

"I do my best."

"If I ever have to have an operation, will you do surgery on me?"

"No, sweetheart. I couldn't ever do surgery on you."

"Why not? I would want you to because you're the best."

"Surgeons can't do operations on their own family."

"Why not?"

Thomas's voice was as calm and gentle as it had been the whole time as he answered. "Because to do a good job as a surgeon, you have to think only about the job, the surgery—not about the person you're working on. And you can't look at your family as a job. You can only look at them as people you love."

"Oh." Mia paused to think some more.

Abigail, deeply touched, moved to the doorway of the kitchen so she could look at them—Thomas with his high forehead and slightly wrinkled dress shirt and Mia with her braids and glasses.

"What if I really need surgery?"

"Then I'll find the best surgeon I can to do it. But I could never look at you as a job."

"So you only look at me as someone you love?" Mia asked.

"That's right. Because you're my daughter, and that's never going to change. No matter what happens to you or to me, no matter what either of us does, I can only look at you as my family, my daughter, as someone I love. I can only look at you as *mine*."

Abigail's eyes burned with emotion at hearing the words, at seeing how much he meant them—even though his matter-of-fact manner had never altered.

Mia nodded, as if she understood and accepted his words. "Then I guess you'll have to find another surgeon as good as you, in case me or Mommy has to have an operation."

Thomas was smiling as Abigail came out feeling strangely overwhelmed with emotion and responding to it by trying to return to normal life. "Okay. I think the game has to be paused for now, or we'll be late for church."

"But I was just getting good at it," Mia complained. "Can we finish after church?"

"It will be bedtime after church, so you'll have to finish it tomorrow. Now run put on your socks and shoes."

Mia didn't look excited, but she wasn't whining as she went to do what she was told.

Thomas had stood up, and Abigail looked up at him for a minute, feeling like he was real to her in a way he hadn't been earlier in their marriage.

"What is it?" he asked, his forehead wrinkling.

She shook her head. "Nothing. Just you were really good with her just now."

"Thank you. Is that all you were thinking?" His eyes were searching her face, and his hand rose to cup her cheek.

It felt like he could read her mind, see how she was feeling, and the idea caused flutters of fear and excitement to rush through her.

If he could see how she was feeling, then he would think they were better, that they were on the cusp of starting again.

Maybe they were.

Maybe after all their work they could finally be rewarded.

Maybe all the work they'd poured into this marriage could finally—finally—be over.

He leaned to kiss her gently, and she clung to him, overwhelmed and bewildered by what seemed to be happening.

"You said we were going to be late for church," Mia said, tying her shoes in the living room.

"We will if we don't leave soon." Abigail said, pulling away from Thomas and flushing from being caught by their daughter.

Thomas chuckled, and Abigail couldn't fail to see that his expression—even beneath his characteristic reserve—was warm, pleased, hopeful.

That made her feel all fluttery too.

∼

The Good Friday service at the church was quiet and solemn. There wasn't much chatting before the service began as the organist played a number of traditional hymns about the crucifixion.

Mia was always good in church because she loved to read, so she sat between her parents with her children's story Bible—with the stories nicely rewritten for children—and read happily. Thomas's arm was across the back of the pew, stretching over Mia's head so his hand was resting on Abigail's shoulders.

She liked it there. She liked how it felt to sit together in the pew. Like a family. Like they'd never been broken.

The service passed with hymns, prayers, readings, a short sermon from Daniel, and then communion. Abigail tried to focus, but she had trouble not thinking about Thomas, about what was happening now between them, about whether she could now let herself hope for the future.

Afterward, after the benediction, groups of the church members had gathered to talk, and Abigail slipped away to go to the bathroom.

She was washing her hands when Lydia came in.

After greeting her sister-in-law, Abigail asked, "When do you all leave for India?"

"Two more months. I'm so excited. You have no idea."

"I think it's amazing the work that you and Gabe are going to do there. Are you nervous?"

Lydia had gone into one of the bathroom stalls, but it didn't stop her from talking. "Occasionally, but not much. I'm just so sure of it, you know."

Abigail sighed. That was the thing. That was why she was still hesitating, no matter how good things were getting between them. She just wasn't sure about her marriage the way Lydia was about India. She stared at her face in the mirror, praying that she would get some sort of sign one way or the other.

She was still standing in front of the sink when Lydia came out to wash her hands.

Giving her a curious look, Lydia asked, "So how are things with you and Thomas?"

"Okay, I guess." Abigail didn't resent the question—since it was characteristic of Lydia's blunt manner—but she wished she had a good answer for her.

"It looks like things are going pretty good." Lydia was obviously trying not to smile too wide. "I mean, I haven't seen Thomas so happy in a really long time. Maybe ever."

Abigail swallowed and stared down at the floor, suddenly feeling guilty for questioning, when it was obvious that Thomas wanted this so much. So did she. "It's complicated," she managed to say.

"I know. I know it takes time, and it's really hard. I'm just really glad..." Lydia cleared her throat. "I'm sorry. Maybe I shouldn't have asked. Thomas is always telling me to back off about it, but I just want you both to be happy."

"I know you do." Abigail smiled, appreciating Lydia's heart despite the uncomfortable feelings the conversation had evoked. "Thank you."

When she left the bathroom, she looked around until she saw Thomas and Mia talking to his parents.

She walked to them automatically, sidestepping to avoid two little boys who were playing in the hall, and she had a strange, sudden recognition.

She'd moved toward Thomas and Mia without even thinking. Because they were her family. Because they were where she belonged.

So she was even more rattled and emotional when she reached them, suddenly wishing she were alone so she could sort through everything she was feeling. Make a wise, conscious decision.

But she wasn't alone. Mia grabbed at her hand, and Thomas wrapped an arm around her, pulling her against his side.

He didn't even seem conscious of doing so. He was focused on talking to his mother about plans for Easter dinner on Sunday. He'd just reached for her. Automatically.

Abigail was so overwhelmed that she could barely have a conversation, but she managed to reply basically coherently when Thomas's mother asked if she could bring some bread to Easter dinner.

Everyone was acting like they were really together again, like it was obvious they'd be coming together here for church on Sunday morning, like there was no question about their relationship.

Abigail had never made a final decision, and the entire world seemed to be turning as if she had.

She should be happy. Of course she should be happy. It was what she'd always wanted—for the endless struggle to finally be over.

But instead she was absolutely terrified.

~

Thomas came into the house with them after they returned home. He helped Abigail pick up the living room as Mia got ready for bed, and then the three of them read several chapters of a book together before they left her room.

Abigail wasn't any more certain or settled than she'd been at church, and it just got worse as Thomas followed her into the kitchen.

He reached into the refrigerator for a half-drunk bottle of wine and poured himself a glass. Then he glanced at her. "You want one?"

"No. Thanks."

He sighed and leaned against the counter, taking a sip and then unbuttoning another button on his dress shirt.

And she realized he wasn't planning to leave. He assumed he would spend the night with her.

It was natural. It was what she'd vaguely been assuming as well.

But he hadn't asked. And she hadn't invited him.

He thought they were fixed now, that they could really be a couple again.

And she still hadn't ever made a decision about that.

Something deep and powerful shuddered through her as Thomas reached over to pull her into a loose embrace. "Are you feeling okay? You look tired."

She was tired, but she was also a lot more than that. And it was all welling up, erupting with the slow, destructive, unstoppable force of a lava flow.

He brushed a few kisses into her hair and then tilted her head up so he could kiss her lips. "Did you want to go to bed early?"

She knew why he wanted to go to bed early. She could feel the tension of arousal start to tighten in his body.

It tightened in hers too, as if her body instinctively responded to his.

It felt right. He was her husband. And he wanted them to be together. She wanted that too.

It felt so *right*.

But it had felt right before too—when she'd given herself to him, trusted him to love and respect and support her, believed he would never hurt her. When he'd believed the same thing about her.

And they had been wrong. They had been broken. They had both felt not good enough, over and over again.

"Not yet," she murmured, trying to talk herself down from the irrational panic.

Things had been going really well. Both of them had grown and changed and were genuinely trying to make this marriage work. Their relationship didn't have to be the way it was before.

She knew—she *knew*—it was true.

They could keep taking it slow. Nothing to get in a panic about.

He settled her into his arms, both of them leaning against the kitchen counter, and he was stroking her hair as he began, "So I was thinking."

Something about his careful tone gave her shivers of worry. "About what?"

"What do you think about the idea of you and Mia moving in with me?"

Her blood seemed to freeze in her veins and then slowly drain out of her face. "I thought we were taking it slow."

"We are," he said quickly. "I'm not rushing you. Just floating the idea out there since things are going so well. It's fine if you're not ready."

He was backpedalling quickly, and she could feel the tension tighten in his body since she was still pressed up against the length of it. She pulled away, the fear and confusion she'd been experiencing all night taking shape and rising up in force. "I'm sorry," she said, her throat closing around the words. "I'm sorry. It's too soon. I'm not ready."

"It's fine. It's fine, Abigail. I'm sorry I asked. It was too soon. I'm really sorry."

He *was* sorry. She could see the emotion twisting on his face. He looked like he'd jumped into full-fledged crisis mode, and she could sense a deep disappointment underlying it because she hadn't responded the way he'd been hoping.

And so she felt guilty. Horribly, achingly guilty. Because she'd hurt him when he'd been trying so hard. Because she couldn't make him happy after all. Because she couldn't get over all their old issues as quickly as she should. Because she wasn't the woman he wanted her to be. She wasn't the wife he really wanted.

And suddenly all of it was happening again—all those feelings of being not good enough, now and so many times in the past.

She experienced again how it had felt when she'd dressed up all sexy for him in lingerie, only for him to reject her. She experienced again how it had felt when she'd showed him a job she'd found that seemed to be made for her, only to end up feeling selfish for even wanting it. She experienced again how it had felt when he'd walked out on her one morning despite her pleas for him to stay because he didn't really want her to be an equal partner in their marriage.

And maybe she knew now why it had happened, why he'd acted the way he did. And maybe she knew how much of the fault had been hers.

But she was back there again—never being good enough, no matter how hard she tried. The old Abigail. The one she'd thought she'd finally overcome.

She would have to fight the whole battle again—and again and again, through the whole of her life. She could see it spread out before her like a vision, all the years, decades, of being trapped in the same cycle.

It was never, ever going to end.

And then it suddenly felt like it had at their last counseling session. The absolute exhaustion from constantly pouring themselves futilely into something that would never be fixed.

She just couldn't do it anymore. She was suddenly every bit as tired as she'd been before Christmas, although she'd thought the exhaustion was over too. She was just so incredibly tired.

It had to finally end.

She stepped away from him abruptly, stumbling backward from the jerky move.

He reached to support her, his face tensing in concern. "What's the matter? Are you okay? I really am sorry. We can pretend I didn't say anything."

She tried to speak but couldn't.

"Abigail?" Thomas's expression was changing, like he had a sudden sense of what was about to happen. "Baby?"

She took a shaky breath. "I think you should go home."

Thomas froze, staring at her blankly.

"I'm sorry," she continued, gripping the edge of the counter. "I'm really sorry, but I think you should go home."

"Okay," he replied, very slowly. "I can go home if you want. But can I please say first that I shouldn't have put pressure on you like that? We'd agreed to take it slow, so it was my fault that I—"

She shook her head, tears burning in her eyes but not falling. "It's not your fault, Thomas. It's not what you said. It just finally all caught up to me. And I don't think I can do this again."

She heard his breath hitch with what felt like tightly repressed emotion.

His voice was slow, careful, gentle as he said, "Things seemed to be going pretty well. If it's not what I just said, then what has happened to make you so scared?"

"Nothing. Not really. It's just too much. For a while, it felt... different, easy. But it's not going to be, is it? And I just can't do all this again. All the hard stuff never ends, and I'm just too tired."

"But it's not going to be like it was before. We've talked about this. It's going to be bet—"

"I don't know if it will be better or not, but that's not really the point. It's *me*. I'm the problem. I just can't do it again."

Thomas was still fully composed, although she knew it was only on the surface. He raised a hand to rub his jaw, and for a moment his eyes were anguished. "Abigail, I don't know what else I can do to show you how much I love you, how sorry I am for the ways I hurt you, how deeply I want to make amends."

She swallowed over a painful lump in her throat and couldn't force out any words.

"Baby, I pushed you away because I was afraid you wouldn't need me anymore, and I'm so sorry for that. I held onto those feelings for way too long. But since Christmas, I've been trying to show you that I love you—exactly as you are—whether you need me or not."

The room started to shudder in front of her eyes.

Thomas continued, "I don't know what else I can do to show you all that, to show you how much I've changed, how much I love you."

She had to turn away from his expression, from the way his voice cracked on the last few words. Her shoulders shook briefly before she was able to say, "It's not you. I'm not expecting you to prove anything to me. This isn't a test or something. It's *me*. I'm the one who's broken. I'm the one who isn't strong enough to go through all the hard stuff again. I'm the one who's too tired to keep fighting for this."

He reached out to touch her arm, but she jerked away from him. "Abigail, please don't say that. I know you're tired. So am I. We've been struggling with this for so long. But we're making progress. And you're not broken."

"Yes, I am! You've spent all this time trying to show me that you love me and Mia, and all I can think about is how I felt when we were together before. Like I was only half a person. Like I was trapped and ashamed and always wrong. Like I was never good enough. I think I've grown and changed since then. God has really been working in my life. And I could feel it just now. Like any moment I might fall back into that old person. And I'll have to fight so hard not to do it."

"I don't want you to be that person either, Abigail. We can work together to make sure neither of us—"

"I know. I know what you're saying is right. But you eventually get to the point where something is so hard, so endlessly hard, that you have to ask yourself whether it's worth fighting for at all. And I don't even know how it happened—why it all caught up to me like this—but it has. I think I've finally gotten there. I'm just not strong enough to do it." Tears were streaming down her face, and she hated herself for them.

Hated herself for the broken expression on Thomas's face too.

Hated herself for everything she had ever done wrong.

Hated herself for never getting any better.

"No one is strong enough. I've really learned this in the past few months too. You're different now because God made you that way. He's made me different too. And he can make our marriage different." Thomas reached out for her. "He can make it new."

She choked on emotion, stepped back from his outstretched hand, and shook her head, blinded by the tears—which was almost a relief because she could no longer see on his face the way she was hurting him. "In heaven, maybe. Maybe then I'll be new. But in this life, it's just battle after battle, and I can't do it anymore."

He started to say something else, but she couldn't let him. She turned her back on him, still clinging to the edge of the counter. "Please, can you just leave? I'm really sorry. I know it's not fair. I know it's hurting you. I know you deserve so much better. But can you please leave now?"

She heard a brief sound—like he was choking, strangled—but he didn't say anything else. Then she heard him walking out of her kitchen, out of her little house, out to his car in the driveway.

It was a year and a half since she'd left him, but it was only this evening that she really knew their marriage was over for good.

ELEVEN

When Abigail glanced in Mia's bedroom, she was relieved to see that the girl had already fallen asleep with a book on her stomach and her glasses still on. Abigail went in to place the book and glasses on the nightstand and turn out the light, glad that her daughter wouldn't see how much she'd been crying in the half hour since Thomas had driven away.

She stood over the bed in the dark room and prayed that Mia wouldn't be hurt by all her mistakes, that her little girl wouldn't suffer for the things that she'd gotten wrong.

Then she was crying again—so hard she had to leave the room.

She cried and prayed for most of the night, and the morning brought neither comfort nor answers.

~

She was such a wreck the next day that, after spending the morning pretending like nothing was wrong so Mia wouldn't be upset, she finally called Lydia to ask if it was all right for Mia to come over to play with Ellie for a couple of hours in the middle of the day. She put on a brave face and avoided any awkward questions when she dropped her daughter off, but Lydia was looking concerned when Abigail drove away.

The whole thing was horrible, and it seemed to affect everyone—like Thomas wasn't the only one whom Abigail had done wrong.

But she just didn't feel strong enough to do anything else.

She went home and stretched out on the couch and turned on the television, hoping to drown out the torrent of pain and confusion in her brain with mindless entertainment. It didn't help though. She lay in a bleak kind of numbness, trying to imagine what it would feel like to be divorced from Thomas completely, for him to no longer be her husband.

She couldn't even imagine it.

She was in such a stupor that she didn't hear the knock on the door for a full minute—not until it was paired with the ringing of the doorbell.

She jumped up, startled and disoriented. No one should be at her door right now, and she wasn't in fit state to see anyone.

But another knock followed, and Abigail had no real choice but to go to the door. Her car was in the driveway. It wasn't like she'd be able to hide.

She opened the door to Jessica, who was holding a casserole dish and smiling a little uncertainly. "Hi," she said. "I don't have to stay. I just wanted to bring you this."

"Oh." Abigail stared at the dish wrapped up with the towel. "What is it?"

"It's my attempt at chicken and rice casserole. I hope it's okay."

"But why..." Abigail didn't finish the question since it should have been self-evident. Jessica was the pastor's wife, and Abigail was at home by herself in sweats and a tear-stained face. "Does everyone know already?" she whispered, horrified by the thought.

"No, no. I'm so sorry." Jessica looked even more worried. "I hope I wasn't too... too presumptuous. Thomas called Daniel this morning. Daniel doesn't tell anyone anything. He doesn't even tell me. But it was a long conversation, and then Daniel seemed... I don't know. And then I talked to Lydia, who was worried that Thomas wasn't answering his phone and that you'd dropped Mia off at her place, so I..." Jessica blew out a breath and looked down at her dish. "Just tell me if I'm being obnoxious, and I promise I'll go. The casserole probably isn't any good, but I thought maybe you wouldn't feel like cooking dinner, so I... Oh, I'm so sorry. Maybe I shouldn't have come."

Abigail had to close her eyes and look away so she wouldn't burst into tears. "Thank you," she said, when she could make her voice work. "You can come in. And I really appreciate the casserole."

Jessica's face reflected obvious relief, and it was a little easier as they went into the kitchen and did normal things like finding a place in the refrigerator for the casserole dish and talk about how Jessica had messed up her first try and had to give most of it to Bear, her dog.

Abigail heated water in the kettle and offered Jessica a cup of tea. She didn't really feel like company, but she wasn't about to return such kindness with a closed door.

"Where's Nathan?" Abigail asked when they both sat down at the dining room table. She'd just realized that it was the first time she'd seen the other woman without her son in the months since he'd been born.

"Daniel is watching him. He's really good with him."

"That's good." Abigail thought about Thomas with Mia, how good a father he'd been trying to be, and her face twisted with suppressed emotion.

Jessica didn't say anything. Didn't ask a question or try to spill out a simplistic moral. She just sat silently and stirred her tea.

Finally Abigail said, "I hate that everyone is going to know."

"Know what?"

"That I gave up on my marriage. That I hurt Thomas and Mia this way."

There was a long pause before Jessica responded. "I don't think anyone can say that you gave up on your marriage. It's been well over a year, and you're still trying to make it work."

"Not anymore," Abigail admitted, feeling a familiar burning in her cheeks. "I gave up last night. I just couldn't do it anymore. I'm just too... too tired. The break was supposed to help, but the tiredness didn't go away."

Jessica took a slow sip of tea. "I can't pretend to know what you're going through. Daniel and I have had our issues, but I know it's not the same. I know it's tempting to stand at a distance and judge other people, assuming there's an easy and obvious answer, but I know it's never that simple. So I'm not likely to have any worthwhile advice, but if you want someone to talk about it to, then you can talk to me."

Abigail opened her mouth to thank the other woman and say no—since her instinct was to never talk about it, never to let anyone know what a mess she really was.

Her parents had always made it very clear that you showed the world nothing but clean hands and face.

But she knew better than that now—no matter what else had happened, she wasn't in that place anymore—so instead of a polite thank you, the words that came out were, "It's not him. It's me."

"What's you?"

"The real problem. I mean, he made mistakes for sure, but he's really been working on them. I'm the one who can't seem to change enough. I... I just know I'm going to feel not good enough again, even when he tries to show me over and over that he doesn't want me to."

Jessica was obviously listening, obviously reflecting on what she'd said, but she didn't jump in with advice or questions.

So Abigail just went on. "I think it's different with me as a mother. I mean, I can fully love Mia and know she loves me. But with Thomas, I kept feeling like I couldn't ever be what he wanted, like he must want something other than me—from the beginning, when I couldn't even… even get through the wedding night. I know in my mind now that it's not true, but I can't seem to not believe it. I thought things were improving and getting easier, but the minute I let my guard down, I start believing it again. I can't seem to change."

Jessica nodded, as if she understood—or as if she at least had heard what Abigail had said.

"So you see, it's not that I can't forgive Thomas. Of course, I can forgive him, just like he's forgiven me. I'm just… so tired. You know, Daniel asked me a while back if I was content to always connect help with shame, and I keep going back to that. Because marriage seems like the most intense version of that feeling. I need Thomas so much—so, so much—and I always feel not good enough with him. Even now, I feel not good enough because I'm not strong enough to be with him the way I should."

Neither of them spoke for a couple of minutes after Abigail had finished. She felt exposed, a little self-conscious, but not the way she normally did when something about her true self was revealed.

"My dad stopped talking to me when I left Thomas," Abigail said, for no particular reason. "He'd been more and more disapproving of the changes I'd made—cutting my hair, changing my clothes, trying to work outside the home. And the separation was the last straw for him. His daughter wouldn't do such a thing, so I must not be his daughter."

"What about your mom?" Jessica asked softly.

Abigail sighed. "She'll never go against my dad. She never did—not once since the day I was born. So I don't talk to her either. Her only act of rebellion is to send me and Mia cards at the holidays. I took Mia up there to try to mend fences over Christmas, and I saw my mother a couple of times, but it didn't fix anything. My father wouldn't even see me. They're ashamed of me." She stared down at the table. "I'm ashamed of myself, but not for the same reasons. It feels like I'm always playing out the same pattern of working so hard to be good enough but never getting there. I just wish I could make myself stop."

"Yeah," Jessica murmured. "It's never that easy."

Abigail felt heard, understood, and not judged at all—which made her feel a little better. She got up to refill their mugs with hot water, and then Jessica said, "I was talking to Daniel earlier this week as he was thinking through his sermon for Good Friday."

Having no idea where this was going, Abigail sat down again, dunking a new tea bag.

"And I was thinking about how what we always think about in Jesus's death is the pain and the blood and the death itself. For good reason, of course, since it was horrible. But as I was talking to Daniel, I had a new thought."

"What thought?" The turn of the conversation seemed safe enough, not horribly painful or intimate, so Abigail was genuinely curious.

"He was naked," Jessica said. "He was *naked*. In front of all those people who hated him. They took his clothes. They utterly humiliated him. He had no dignity or privacy or security left. They took it all. And I kept thinking, that's our shame. That's *my* shame. He carried that too."

She didn't even seem to be talking to Abigail anymore. She was staring down at her tea, murmuring almost to herself, "To make us new. To make us beautiful."

Abigail felt frozen, almost numb, as she processed the words, as she understood them as true. She couldn't say anything, couldn't react in any appropriate way. She just sat, something inside her shaking helplessly.

"Anyway," Jessica said, wiping a tear away with an ironic sigh. "I'm not any good at advice or comforting words, but that's what I was thinking."

Abigail tried to say something, but couldn't.

"Are you okay?" Jessica asked, after another minute.

Abigail shook her head. "I don't think I am."

"Well, just let me know if you need anything. And if you ever need some time on your own or decide you want to talk to Thomas or anything, you're welcome to drop Mia off with me. Mia and I had a long conversation on Friday evening about what kinds of books I should get to read to Nathan, so I think we get along pretty well."

Abigail felt a ripple of amusement, picturing Mia's grave face during the conversation, and the brief laughter seemed to crack something inside her, a well of feeling that could barely be held back.

Jessica was already on her way out, and she didn't linger for more conversation. Abigail did her best to thank her, but she was close to sobbing as she finally closed the door.

She leaned against the door, her whole body shaking, sinking down to the floor and hugging her knees as the emotion rocked her, as she saw her whole history of never feeling good enough illuminated by the truth.

It was a long time before she could stand up again.

~

She eventually pulled herself together enough to pick up Mia, and they went out to get ice cream and took it to the duck pond so they could sit on a bench as they ate it.

Mia liked to watch the ducks, and Abigail just wanted to occupy her mind so she wouldn't start crying again.

After they scraped the last of the ice cream from their cups, Mia stared out at the pond for a long time, finally asking, "Is Daddy coming over tonight?"

With a painful slice through her heart, Abigail said, "I don't think so, honey."

"Did you guys have a bad fight?"

"We didn't have a fight. You know that he doesn't come over every night."

"But he's been coming a lot. And he's been kissing you and sleeping over. I thought maybe we would all live together again."

Abigail pulled the girl closer, wrapping her in a hug. "I'm sorry, honey. I don't know if that will happen."

"Grown up stuff is complicated," Mia said with a sigh, repeating words she'd heard many times.

"It is. But we both love you so much. You know that, don't you?"

Mia nodded, no uncertainty at all on her face. "Yes, I know that. But you don't love each other?"

"Yes, we love each other. We do. But that doesn't mean we're going to live together again."

"I wanted us to. I wanted us all to move into Daddy's house with all the trees and the window seat for reading."

Abigail stroked loose strands of hair from her face. "I know. That does sound nice, doesn't it? But our home is nice too, isn't it?"

"Yes. It is."

Mia didn't say anything else immediately, but Abigail knew it was because she was thinking things through. She was like Thomas in that—sorting ideas out in her mind before she had them together enough to put into words.

Abigail waited patiently, staring out at the rippling water of the pond. When Mia's thinking went on for much longer than normal, she started to get worried though. So she finally asked, "Are you okay, Mia? I know you wanted Daddy around all the time, but I promise it will still be okay."

Mia nodded gravely. "Yes. It's okay. It's like Daddy said."

"What did Daddy say?"

"He said he looks at me and loves me no matter what happens. Even if I'm sick or I'm bad or anything. Because I'm his. He looks at us and loves us. It's that way with us and Daddy, right? We look at him and love him—even if he's crabby from work or not living with us—because he's ours."

"Yes," Abigail said slowly, the emotion that had been so close to the surface all day rising up again at the sweet words. "That's exactly right."

She hugged Mia close, fighting back the burning in her eyes since she didn't want to cry and scare the little girl.

And when Mia got up and went to throw away their empty cups, Abigail suddenly knew exactly what she needed to do.

Mia had been exactly right. Abigail looked at Thomas and loved him. Still. No matter how much work it might still take to make their marriage what it should be. And she suddenly knew—knew without any doubt or question—that Thomas looked at her and loved her too.

~

Abigail had to call Jessica up and ask if Mia could come visit Nathan for an hour or two so she could go talk to Thomas. Mia wanted to come to see her father too, but Abigail knew they could never have the conversation they needed if their daughter was present, so she promised to bring Daddy back with her if at all possible.

This seemed to satisfy Mia, who was excited about seeing baby Nathan and talking to Jessica about books. If Jessica knew what was happening—as she almost certainly did—she never revealed a clue, just acted casual and friendly as she and Bear welcomed Mia inside.

Abigail drove over to Thomas's house, a big, rambling Victorian on several acres. She parked in the driveway and sat staring at the front door, trying to work up the courage to go knock.

Now that she was here, she was terrified again. She'd hurt Thomas. A lot. Evidently, he hadn't been answering his phone, even when his sister tried to call him. He'd poured so much into their relationship over the past few months, and she'd rewarded it with nothing but a broken heart. Eventually, he would give up and find someone who treated him better.

She fought against the feelings though, knowing they weren't based in truth, and she made herself get out of the car and walk up the door. She rang the doorbell. Then waited, hugging her arms to her chest.

After a minute, she heard slow steps coming toward the door, creaking on the old hardwood of the front hall.

Then there was a pause. He probably looked out to see who it was.

Then suddenly the door swung open so quickly it left her breathless.

Thomas stared at her. He wore a T-shirt and the bunny pajama pants that Mia had picked out for him, and his face was stretched far more than normal, dark shadows under his eyes.

He didn't look like he'd slept at all. He looked terrible and wonderful and exactly like Thomas. Every feeling and instinct in her body and heart reached out toward him in absolute need.

"Hi," she said stupidly, when he kept staring at her in silence.

His eyes moved over her shoulder, to her car, and then back up the walk to her face again—like he was checking to see if Mia was present.

"She's at Jessica and Daniel's," Abigail explained. "So I could come talk to you."

Thomas's frozen composure cracked then. She could see it quite clearly. It cracked just like the flood of her own emotions had cracked earlier when she'd been talking to Jessica.

He made a rough, guttural sound, his face almost contorting with powerful feeling, and he reached out to pull her into his arms.

She wrapped her arms around him, holding him as tightly as he held her, and he was real and warm and strong and weak and human. He was *Thomas*.

"Oh, baby," he murmured, his face buried in her hair. "I'm so sorry if I pressured you or tried to push you into something too fast."

"You didn't—"

"I know I did. I was just so excited. I've wanted you back so much for so long that I wasn't thinking about how fast we were moving. But I promise I can be patient. I'll wait just as long as you need. I'm not expecting any sort of final answer or commitment, but please say you won't give up on us completely. I know how hard it is. I know how tired we both still are. I know it can't all be fixed just because we both might want it to be. I can wait however long you need. I love you, baby. I *love* you, and that's never going to change."

He'd finally loosened his grip and pulled back, but only to take her face in both of his hands. "I want you to believe me one day. I want you to know for sure how strong and sweet and brave and beautiful you are to me. But if you don't, I'll still love you. Nothing is going to make me stop."

She raised her hands to cover his on her face and was momentarily blinded by tears. "I do believe you," she managed to choke out. "I do believe you. I love you too."

He looked like someone had socked him in the gut—absolutely dumbfounded.

"I love you, Thomas," she said again, lowering his hands from her face and taking both of them in hers. "I still love you. I never stopped. And I know I'm too tired and not strong enough to fight all my old struggles, but the real fight has already been won. And the rest I don't have to do alone. I know that now. I think I finally... I finally see it. So I want to love you all the way. If you'll help me. If you'll do it with me. If we can really do this together. That's what I came over here to say."

When the words finally processed, he made another one of those strangled sounds and gathered her into his arms again.

Since she hadn't quite finished, she said against his shirt, "I know we still have some work to do. I know we're never going to be perfectly fixed, so I need to stop expecting that. We can still go to counseling for a while, if that's okay with you. But I want to be your wife again. All the way. I want us to live together again. I love you, and you love me, and I want to finally live that out."

He was shuddering against her, beneath her hands. She'd never once in her life seen him like this—so absolutely discomposed.

If she hadn't known it before, there was no way to deny it now. This man felt deeply. He loved deeply. And all the depth and power of his passion and devotion was focused on her, was given to her, was spread like a benediction over *her*.

TWELVE

When the hug finally ended, Thomas still stood in the doorway, gazing down at her. At long last, they seemed to understand each other.

Finally, Thomas said, "Did you want to come in and talk about it?"

"Yeah. I do. But before that, do you think maybe you could kiss me?"

There had been a lilt to her tone, so Thomas was chuckling warmly as he pulled her into the house, closed the door behind them, then leaned down and claimed her mouth.

Abigail instinctively twined her arms around his neck, holding his head in place with one hand. He slid his tongue along the line of her lips until she opened for him. Then his tongue met hers, and Abigail groaned into his mouth at the resulting sensations and feelings.

It felt real, completely, like a concrete manifestation of how they were really together again.

The kiss got really deep really fast since both of them were pretty stretched in their emotions. Soon Abigail could feel Thomas's hard arousal rubbing against her, and her own body was squirming with increasing urgency.

When Thomas finally tore his mouth away from hers, he panted a few times. "Did you want to talk now?"

She assessed the state of her heart and her body and said hoarsely, "We can if you want. Or we can... do something else first."

"Do we need to get Mia anytime soon?"

"No. Jessica said she could stay for a few hours."

His skin was slightly damp, and he rubbed his forehead. "I don't want to pressure you to anything too soon, but do you think—"

"Thomas," she said, interrupting. "Of course, we can have sex. What did you think I meant by something else. I'm your wife, and I'm dying to."

He let out his breath in a rush, his face transforming with relief. "Then shall we go upstairs? Because honestly, if we don't, I might just lose it right here in the entry hall."

She giggled helplessly and then let him grab her hand as they both hurried up the stairs to his bedroom.

There, he kissed her again and then swung her down onto the bed, causing a thrill of excitement to run through her, a top note to the current of deep emotion.

When he moved over her, Abigail felt another thrill, this time centered in a very specific location. She maneuvered her legs so that her thighs were on either side of his hips.

When Thomas just gazed at her again, she said, "I thought you wanted to make love."

"I do. You better believe I do."

"You're just staring at me."

"I can't help it. I feel like a miracle happened, like the world just came back to life."

She wrapped her arms around him, pulling him down into a kiss. "Maybe it did."

Thomas kissed her with slow, sensual care. The press of his hot, hard body was delicious, and the vibrations from his suppressed laughter and emotion generated shivers of pleasure shooting down to her growing arousal.

Abigail tried to stroke his hair with her fingertips, but as the swell of excitement built inside her, she ended up clutching more than caressing.

Her feelings were just too powerful to contain.

By the time his tongue had thoroughly explored her mouth and teased her tongue into fluttering, Abigail was making smothered moans in the back of her throat and arching up to rub herself against him. "Thomas, please don't stall."

"I'm not stalling, baby. I'm trying to contain myself so I don't totally lose it. But I promise I'll give you anything you want."

Abigail's breathing sped up to shallow pants as he took off her clothes, tenderly kissing the skin that was revealed. Then she gave a little squeak of pleasure when he mouthed just beneath her belly button. Her blood was coursing through her heated body, and her mind was clouding with desire. He was pressing kisses on different spots of her stomach—each perfectly placed to both surprise and stimulate her.

Thomas mouthed one of her breasts, and then he flicked his tongue, making her jerk up her knee. "So beautiful."

"I love you, Thomas." Abigail gasped, almost writhing as he twirled her nipple with his tongue and his lips. "So much."

Thomas lowered his head again to give her breasts more attention. Soon, she was biting her lip to keep from moaning too loudly as he suckled one breast with his mouth and fondled the other with his hand.

She was bucking up her hips involuntarily, trying to get some friction against her throbbing arousal. She knew Thomas was aroused too—he'd been aroused from the beginning—but he was tightly controlling himself, and he hadn't yet lost his restraint.

When she started clawing at his back through his shirt, Abigail finally panted, "Thomas! I'm turned on. You're killing me now."

Thomas raised his head to look up at her flushed, damp face, and Abigail took advantage of his distraction to grab fistfuls of his shirt so she could pull it off over his head.

He raised his hands to help her get it off. "I want it to be really good for you," he murmured, his gaze so hot and tender that she wanted to melt into the bed.

His words and the sentiment touched her deeply, but a sliver of irony rose up, prompting her to say, "Well, if you don't get moving, I'm going to take matters in hand, and it's going to be good for me all by myself."

He stifled a burst of laughter and pulled her up into an embrace. After kissing her hard and deep, he mouthed a wet trail along her jaw and to her ear. "Keep making me laugh like that," he murmured thickly, "And we might have an unfortunate incident."

Abigail was torn between appreciative laughter and a secret thrill of delight. She knew Thomas was teasing, but he wouldn't have teased about it unless his declining control was really an issue.

And the thought that Thomas was so affected by her was the deepest kind of aphrodisiac.

Thomas had shifted his position above her, so that the hard bulge in his pants was in line with her groin. She folded her legs up on either side of his hips. She whimpered at the stimulation and started to grind against him urgently.

"Fuck!" Thomas gasped, straightening his arms and holding himself still. His features were twisted with effort. "Abigail, baby, I wasn't kidding."

She stopped rubbing against him and just stared up at his damp face, her mind whirling with the sensations and with what Thomas had just revealed.

"Sorry." Her hands settled on his shoulders and she smiled up at him shyly. "I didn't mean to."

He chuckled again—thick and hoarse—and then he leaned down to kiss her. "You can do whatever you want. I just wanted you to know there might be consequences."

She giggled at his wry tone. "An unfortunate incident."

"It is a possibility. It's been a really long couple of days," he admitted.

Abigail's face softened. "I know. I'm sorry."

He shook his head. "Don't. We're together now. We're not looking back."

Abigail reached over to push down his flannel pants until he was as naked as she was. Then she spread her thighs to make room for him between them, weaving her fingers together at the back of his neck.

After giving her another quick kiss, Thomas reached down and slid two of his fingers against her hot, aroused flesh. Abigail sucked in her breath. Then gave a little moan as he sunk his fingers inside her.

Having determined that she was ready for him, Thomas pulled his fingers out and lined his erection up at her entrance.

Then, with a rock of his hips, he slid himself in, the substance of him pushing into the very tight clasp of her body.

Abigail grunted and arched her back up, her arms flying out to clutch at the blanket beneath her as he pushed in more deeply.

"Abigail," Thomas rasped, his body tensing dramatically and his head jerking to the side. "Oh, fuck."

Breathing deeply and relaxing around him, Abigail desperately hoped he wasn't going to lose it.

It might be thrilling that he wanted her so much, but it would be a bit of a letdown if it was over before it started.

He was breathing through his nose so heavily his nostrils were flaring. But after a minute he looked back down at her questioning face and anxious eyes. "No worries. You can move now."

She couldn't stifle a relieved chuckle. "Oh, good." She adjusted her legs, and reached up to hold on to his bare shoulders.

"I think it's the overload of emotion." He shifted his knees, which caused his erection to slide inside her a little. Then his mouth twitched slightly. "I'm usually a man of iron control."

Abigail stroked his face tenderly "I know."

Thomas braced himself on his arms, and his expression changed—grew both hot and focused. Abigail felt her arousal pulsing again, intensified by the solid feel of him inside her.

Responding to her implicit challenge, Thomas pulled his pelvis back until only the tip of his erection was inside her. Then he thrust back in, with a long, tight slide.

Hissing in a breath, Abigail arched her neck and closed her eyes, trying to concentrate on the delicious sensations.

Thomas pulled back again and gave another long thrust, the push of his hard flesh stimulating her inner walls on both the withdrawal and the advance.

"So good," she breathed as he continued, rocking her hips up to meet each of his thrusts. It felt right and good and somehow freeing. As if was really her, and he was really Thomas—their real selves and not the masks they put on.

Thomas's eyes were devouring her face, her naked breasts, and her sprawled hair. "You're so beautiful, baby. I've never wanted anyone but you."

Abigail whimpered in response, feeling almost as much from his gaze and his voice as she was from the motion of him inside her. "I've never wanted anyone but you either."

Thomas's tense face broke into a smile, and he reared up even farther, changing the angle of his penetration.

Abigail cried out in startled pleasure and let go of his shoulders again, her arms going above her head and fumbling for purchase on the pillow.

Thomas was so tight that the muscles in his chest and arms were visibly clenched. He was watching her with heated possession. "Can you come, baby?"

Abigail almost sobbed as the pleasure became torturous because she couldn't quite find her release. "Think so." She panted.

She managed to focus enough to move one of her arms down and squeeze her hand between their bellies. Thomas had to pull up even farther, but she fumbled around near where they were connected—brushing her knuckles against the base of Thomas's shaft—until she was able to press two fingertips against her clit.

As soon as she rubbed a tight circle, she felt a rush of relieving pleasure.

Perspiration was running down the side of his face now, and all his features were rigid with effort except his eyes—which were still raking over her. "Come, baby. Come."

Her voice was almost embarrassingly shrill, but she couldn't care as her orgasm began to overwhelm her. "Thomas!"

She came on the word, her body starting to convulse as all the luscious pressure was finally released inside her.

"Fuck." Thomas grunted, thrusting with primitive urgency into her clenching muscles in short, rapid strokes. "Abigail, baby."

She was coming down from her climax, just as Thomas was finally letting go. So she held on to him with her legs and her free arm and gazed up at his tense face.

It took him a minute before he could release the last thread of his control, and there was something incongruously intimate about holding him like this, watching him take pleasure in her so visibly, nakedly.

His pelvis jerked erratically—having totally fallen out of rhythm—and it felt like inside was swelling inside the tightened clasp of her channel. Then his twisting features abruptly transformed in a rush of tangible relief.

He froze on a muffled, incoherent exclamation. Then gave a few, hard, spasmodic jerks inside her.

Then he was coming, moaning hoarsely as he gave into his release.

Her eyes were burning, and for some reason Abigail felt almost as affected by watching him come as she'd been from coming herself. She pulled her hand out from between their bodies and wrapped both of her arms around him, holding him with strong urgency as she felt him finally begin to relax.

He bent his arms and folded his forearms beneath her shoulders so he could return her embrace.

He didn't say anything. Neither did she. They both just gasped and clutched at the other, and Thomas lowered his head until he was breathing hotly against her hair.

And she felt whole then. Like *they* were whole. Like they were really one.

And she managed to say with the last of her breath, "Do you have any idea how much I love you?"

He smiled and said, "I do."

～

They went to pick up Mia when they pulled themselves together, and all of them went out for an early dinner.

Mia was obviously thrilled to see that Thomas was with them, but she didn't ask any questions about why he was there or what had happened between them.

Maybe things were simpler for her, or maybe she was just waiting to see what happened. It was hard to tell with Mia.

They went back to the little house after dinner, and they all piled in Abigail's bed to watch a movie and then read.

And Abigail couldn't remember ever being happier, feeling more like a family.

It was after nine when Mia finally went to bed. She wasn't too happy about bedtime, but Abigail told her she needed to get some good sleep since tomorrow was Easter.

Thomas asked what Mia was most looking forward to about Easter, and the girl thought for a long time and said it was a tie between wearing her new dress and singing her favorite hymn with all the alleluias and knowing that Jesus had risen from the dead. He stroked her hair and told her they were all good things, but the last was most important.

He told her that Easter was about hope and victory and new life—the sign that what was wrong with the world would one day finally be fixed.

She nodded gravely and leaned up for her bedtime kisses from both of them. And as they were leaving the room, she asked, "Like us?"

"Like us what?" Thomas asked, turning around.

"Being fixed. Us as a family. We were fixed because of Easter?"

"Yes," Thomas said, his eyes meeting Abigail's in the dim light of the room. "That's right."

∼

The next morning, the three of them went to the sunrise service, which was held outside on the lawns of the church, from which there was a view of the sun rising from behind the mountains through the clouds in a splendor of orange and purple.

The morning was chilly, and Abigail and Mia were wearing thick sweaters over their Easter dresses, but they still huddled together for warmth.

Abigail felt overly emotional as she sang and prayed, her arm around Mia and Thomas's arm around both of them.

She listened to Daniel talk about the resurrection as being so full of hope and joy because suffering and death are so real and powerful in the world.

And it felt to her, standing there with Thomas and Mia, that their marriage, their family, might be full of even more hope and joy because they'd both worked so hard to get here.

There would be more work—some of it excruciating—and more joy too. Both of them a kind of gift.

Afterward, they all went back to the church building to have breakfast before the regular church service.

Lydia ran over to hug them all with obvious delight and excitement, and Jessica and Daniel were both beaming when they looked in her direction. It didn't even make Abigail feel self-conscious.

It seemed natural for others to be happy for them—to be happy that what was broken could eventually be mended.

She wanted to be part of this church, have these people as part of her life and the life of her family. They probably didn't understand everything that she and Thomas had been through—who could if they didn't live through it themselves?—but these people seemed to care about both of them, feel with and for both of them.

And she realized with a pang of surprise that she wasn't even assuming they were judging her for all the mistakes she had made.

After the breakfast was over and people were cleaning up, Abigail noticed Sophie Miller in a corner on her own, wiping down one of the tables.

Abigail went over to say hello since she hadn't seen Sophie since the book club except just in passing.

Sophie smiled, looking lovely in a pale blue dress but with a kind of loneliness under the surface.

Abigail started helping by straightening the chairs around the table that Sophie was wiping. "Do you have plans for dinner today?" she asked, thinking that maybe they could invite Sophie over if she wasn't already doing something.

They were having dinner with Thomas's parents and Lydia, Gabe, and Ellie, but she didn't think anyone would mind an extra.

"Yeah," Sophie said with a smile. "The Duncans invited me over."

"Oh, good. Maybe we could have lunch sometime in the next week or two," Abigail suggested, the idea coming to her spontaneously. "I'm going to start coming to church here now, and I wanted to get to know some more people."

"I'd like that," Sophie said with a smile. "I'm glad things are going better with..." She trailed off, but completed the thought by nodding toward Thomas, who was having an earnest conversation with Mia and Ellie.

"Yeah," Abigail said, feeling a rush of pleasure at the knowledge that the other woman's observation was true. They didn't just look like they were doing better. They *were* doing better. "We're still working on things, but we're... we're happy too."

Then she remembered that Sophie's situation wasn't nearly as hopeful as hers was. "I guess you get tired of people asking you if there's any news about Mark," she said.

Sophie nodded with a dry smile. "It was really bad at the beginning. No one could seem to talk to me about anything else. But no one asks anymore. I think they're afraid of hearing the answer—that they've given up hope."

"But you haven't given up hope, have you? Prisoners do get returned from... from situations like that, don't they?"

"Not always, but they sometimes do. It's just a matter of when. I can't even imagine what he's going through. It's going to have changed him so much. I'm not even sure I'll know him when he comes home."

She'd said something similar the day of the book club, and Abigail could completely understand why. "Yeah," she murmured, not even sure how to answer the poignancy of the words. "I can see that."

Sophie smiled, her face clearing. "What about Thursday for lunch? Does that work for you?"

Abigail thought quickly over her schedule before saying that Thursday worked fine.

∼

Dinner lasted for a long time—between the preparation, eating, and aftermath—so it was late afternoon when things finally started to wind down.

Mia and Ellie wanted to play outside at Thomas's parents' house, so Abigail went out with the girls since Thomas and Gabe were in the middle of a conversation about local politics and the others were working in the kitchen.

Abigail had had a really good day. She felt tired and incredibly hopeful. It felt like she was really part of this family.

But it made her think about her own parents, about the Easter card her mother had sent her—signed simply, "Love, Mom."

Sitting on one of the deck chairs, watching the girls play, Abigail finally pulled out her phone and stared down at it.

She stared for so long and with such focus that she gave a little start when she heard a voice behind her.

"Is everything all right?"

She looked up to see Thomas. She couldn't help but smile at the sight of him, at the knowledge that they were together again, that they really heard and understood each other at last.

"Yeah." She waited until Thomas had taken the seat next to hers on the deck. "I was actually trying to get the courage up to call my mom."

He looked surprised. "Really? Do you think she'll talk to you?"

"I don't know. If my dad is around, probably not. But I feel like I want to try. I don't know—I just don't like to leave it broken that way. You and I were able to work through things, so that gives me hope that maybe... I don't know."

"It can't hurt to try," he murmured.

It could hurt. It would hurt if her mother hung up on her. It would hurt a lot. But she knew what Thomas was saying.

She nodded, praying silently as she worked up the last of her courage. "Okay. I'm going to do it."

"Do you want me to leave?"

She shook her head. "It will help if you're here."

She saw the words wash over Thomas's face and realized they meant something to him.

She couldn't let that distract her though as she scrolled for her parents' number.

As the phone rang, Thomas reached over and took her hand.

He held it as she waited, and as her mother's soft voice came on the line.

The conversation lasted only three minutes—mostly just happy Easters and some news about Mia. Thomas held her hand the whole time.

Her father obviously didn't want to talk to her, but her mother didn't hang up.

So that felt like a victory too.

~

They spent the night at Thomas's house. It was going to be their house soon since Abigail and Mia were going to give up their little rented bungalow and move in with him.

It already felt like their home as they piled up on the couch together to read a book out loud. They were reading *Little Men* now, which Mia liked even better than *Little Women*, although they had to fill her in on the backstory from the second half of the previous book.

When they put Mia to bed, they came back to the living room and Thomas collapsed on the couch, sprawled out the whole length of it.

Abigail smiled down at him, feeling rather sappy. He looked absolutely exhausted—which was a characteristic Thomas look. But he also looked happy.

So happy.

And she felt so pleased and proud and overwhelmed that she was part of why he was so happy.

He reached an arm out toward her, and she came to him willingly, letting him settle her half beside and half on top of him—both of them stretched out on the couch.

"I love you," he murmured, brushing a kiss into her hair.

She smiled against his chest. "I love you too."

"And I feel like I finally know what it means to love. It took me a long time to figure it out."

"Me too," she admitted, tilting her head so she could see his face. "Me too."

"I'm not saying I've got it all together and have everything fixed like I thought I had before," he added, a different note in his voice. "I can't believe I was so arrogant back then. I know I'll still need to—"

"I know," she said, interrupting, smiling at him rather mushily. "I know exactly what you mean. That's how I feel too. It won't all be easy, but we'll keep working on it. It just finally feels like it will be worth it. That there's joy as well as effort."

He adjusted so he could kiss her softly on the lips. "So much joy."

When the kissed deepened into something that was clearly turning into sex, Abigail pulled away slightly. "If we keep doing this without protection, then Mia's going to eventually have a little brother or sister."

She felt Thomas's reaction in his body. "I've still got condoms we can use. I don't want to rush you into anything."

She felt a smile warming her all over. "Does that mean you want another baby?"

He lifted himself up enough so they could have a real conversation. His expression was just slightly sheepish. "I wouldn't be... disappointed if that were to happen. But I was serious about not rushing you or assuming you want the same things I do. Having another baby would make things more complicated—in terms of logistics of our jobs and such—so we need to work out whether we want that and then the timing together."

For some reason, the earnest words filled her with such a wave of affection that she couldn't begin to contain it. She grabbed him and pulled him down into a tight hug.

He hugged her back, and his voice was confused and laughing both as he said, "Was that an answer?"

"Yes, it was an answer. I want us to work it out together too. And the truth is I would love to have another baby with you. I always kind of wanted one. In fact, I'm ready now, if you are."

For a moment, it looked like the joy on Thomas's face would actually crack, but then his expression transformed to his typical warm intelligence. "Well, that might have been the easiest decision that we've ever worked out."

She laughed as he hugged her again, and then she grabbed his face to kiss him.

Thomas had always been a hard worker. His parents and Lydia had been laughing over lunch about how consumed he'd been in high school at preparing for his chess tournaments. He clearly hadn't changed in that regard.

Because right now he wasted no time in getting hard at work on baby making.

ABOUT NOELLE ADAMS

Noelle handwrote her first romance novel in a spiral-bound notebook when she was twelve, and she hasn't stopped writing since. She has lived in eight different states and currently resides in Virginia, where she writes full time, reads any book she can get her hands on, and offers tribute to a very spoiled cocker spaniel.

She loves travel, art, history, and ice cream. After spending far too many years of her life in graduate school, she has decided to reorient her priorities and focus on writing contemporary romances. For more information, please check out her website: noelle-adams.com.

Books by Noelle Adams

Beaufort Brides Series
> Hired Bride
> Substitute Bride
> Accidental Bride

One Night Novellas
> One Hot Night: 3 Contemporary Romance Novellas
> One Night with her Boss
> One Night with her Roommate
> One Night with the Best Man

Willow Park Series
> Married for Christmas

A Baby for Easter
A Family for Christmas
Reconciled for Easter
Home for Christmas

Heirs of Damon Series
Seducing the Enemy
Playing the Playboy
Engaging the Boss
Stripping the Billionaire

Standalones
A Negotiated Marriage
Listed
Bittersweet
Missing
Revival
Holiday Heat
Salvation
Excavated
Overexposed
Road Tripping

The Protectors Series (co-written with Samantha Chase)
Duty Bound
Honor Bound
Forever Bound
Home Bound

Made in the USA
Middletown, DE
09 August 2016